Invincible
The Trident Code: Book 1

Alana Albertson

Bolero Books, LLC
POWAY, CALIFORNIA

Copyright © 2014 by Alana Albertson.

All rights reserved. No part of this publication may be reproduced, distributed or transmitted in any form or by any means, including photocopying, recording, or other electronic or mechanical methods, without the prior written permission of the publisher, except in the case of brief quotations embodied in critical reviews and certain other noncommercial uses permitted by copyright law. For permission requests, write to the publisher, addressed "Attention: Permissions Coordinator," at the address below.

Bolero Books, LLC
11956 Bernardo Plaza Dr. #510
San Diego, CA 92128
www.buybolerobooks.com

Publisher's Note: This is a work of fiction. Names, characters, places, and incidents are a product of the author's imagination. Locales and public names are sometimes used for atmospheric purposes. Any resemblance to actual people, living or dead, or to businesses, companies, events, institutions, or locales is completely coincidental.

Book Layout & Design ©2014 - BookDesignTemplates.com
Cover Design by Regina Wamba – Mae I Design

Ordering Information:
Quantity sales. Special discounts are available on quantity purchases by corporations, associations, and others. For details, contact the "Special Sales Department" at the address above.

Invincible/ Alana Albertson. – 2nd ed.
ISBN 978-1-941665-92-3

*This book is dedicated to all the women in the world who have been trafficked.
May they have hope and find peace.*

We are U.S. Navy SEALs.
There's no need to thank us because we don't exist.
You never saw us.
This never happened.

–ANONYMOUS

Acknowledgements

I would like to thank the love of my life, my husband, Roger, a real Marine hero. Thank you for being such a wonderful husband to me and the best daddy to our sons. For watching the boys while I write. For keeping me caffeinated during late night writing sessions. I love you.

To Nicole Blanchard. This book would not have been written without you. For your initial blurb challenge, to your endless tolerance for my what ifs, your social media prowess, and for your pep talks at the wee hours in the morning when I was determined to give up and unpublish. But mostly for being such an amazing woman and friend.

I would like to thank my editors for turning this book into what it was meant to be.
Megan McKeever—for convincing me to give Annie her voice back.
Karen Dale Harris—for your insight into Patrick's characterization.
Hot Tree Editing—Jennifer and Becky for your passion about Invincible. And to their betas, Sue and Teri.
Deborah Halverson—for your initial support and insight for this project.
Carol Agnew—for your amazing proofing.
To my two beautiful sons, Connor and Caleb for your smiles, your laughter, your hugs and kisses.

To my cover designer: Regina Wamba for bringing Pat and Annie to life.

To my betas: Erin, Mia, Geri, Margreet, Stacia, Linda, and Carly: thank you all for your honest critiques and making this the best story it could be.

My sister-in-law Susie Chulick, for staying positive and encouraging me not to give up on this book.

To my insanely talented audio team: Grant George for making Pat, Kyle and Vic sexy and tough. Alexa Kahn for giving Annie strength and levity, and Erick Cifuentes for your astute producing and editing skills.

To all the wonderful bloggers who have promoted Invincible: Totally Booked, Aestas, Sinfully Sexy, Lezley-Lynn's Book Blog, Romance Vault, Sassy Bookista, Eye Candy, Muses Circle, and the countless others that have posted about my book.

To Indie Sage Promotions for handling all the promotion for the book.

To all the fans who have written me about Invincible. Thank you for all your support.

Invincible

I'LL BE HONEST WITH YOU. I'll be honest with you—I'm no hero. Sure, the media tries to brand every Navy SEAL as some kind of Batman dressed in cammies. There's even a line in one of our cadences: Superman is the man of steel, he ain't no match for Navy SEAL. You've seen the movies—we're infallible, invaluable, invincible. But that night, the one you read about in the papers ... all I really wanted to do was get laid.

One harmless fuck with an Aruban whore, no strings attached. I picked her out of a lineup—wild, dark hair, long legs and a crooked smile. After she sucked me off, I relaxed back onto the creaky, cum-stained cot, thankful for the blissful moments she gave me when I actually forgot for a second the faces of my buddies who died because I made the wrong call, the tears of the children I couldn't save, and the eyes of the enemies I slaughtered during their last seconds of life.

But before I left, her hazel eyes peered into my soul. She whispered in a distinct Californian accent, "My name is Annie Hamilton. I'm an American citizen. I was kidnapped on spring break five years ago. You're my last hope. Please save me."

One desperate plea. This wasn't a Hollywood blockbuster or a New York Times best-selling thriller. I knew this time there was no room for excuses, no margin for errors. I had one chance to put on the cape and be her hero.

1. Patrick

LIBERTY. FINALLY, A NIGHT OFF. Fuck yeah!
Petty Officer 2nd Class Victor Gonzales slicked some gel into his dark brown hair and slathered on some after-shave. "Hey, Walsh—you wanna go to that club tonight? Near the plaza?"

Another tourist hotspot in picturesque Aruba—drunken college girls on spring break, wayward daughters escaping their parents on family vacations. I had no desire to spend my first night on land in six months making small talk, hoping to get lucky. I wanted a sure thing, with no strings.

"No thanks, man. I'm just going to head on into town and get a bite to eat." S `

Lieutenant Commander Kyle Lawson trimmed his short black beard and nodded toward me. "You sure? You're my wingman, bro. Vic over here can never close the deal."

Vic threw the bottle of hair gel at Kyle. "Fuck you, Kyle. I have standards—I don't just sleep with every girl who says hi to me."

Yeah, I definitely needed to go solo tonight, even though the three of us always made our mark when we hit the town. Three United States Navy SEALs didn't exactly blend in with the local tourists. We were all ripped, especially since on deployment we spent all our free time in the ship's gym. Vic's huge arms were decorated with tattoos. Stupid motherfucker, identifying markers weren't a plus in the Teams. He'd never make SEAL Team Six. And at six feet five inches tall, former NFL linebacker Kyle towered over Vic and me, though we could hardly be considered short since we both measured in at over six feet. People would stop Kyle all the time and ask him for an autograph, confusing him with a Hollywood movie star or a rapper. Not to mention, the two of them looked like a walking Navy SEAL diversity outreach recruitment poster, with me standing out as the blond-haired, blue-eyed boy.

"I'll meet up with you two fools later." For the past six months, I'd spent every waking minute with my Team—SEAL Team Seven to be precise. We'd been circling the Caribbean Islands, working our asses off, patrolling and hunting "go-fast" boats run by South American drug cartels. Tomorrow, I planned to snorkel, relax on the beach, and rest before we returned home from deployment. And later tonight I'd meet up with Kyle and Vic and get hammered.

But first things first—I needed some pussy.

I pulled on my civilian clothes, which felt foreign to my body. Sandals and shorts instead of boots and "utes." I glanced in the mirror and debated whether to shave off my full beard. No point. One benefit of being a SEAL was our relaxed grooming standards. The Marines on our carrier still had to shave daily and cut their hair within regulation. We SEALs could grow full beards and keep our hair longer, to blend in undercover. I certainly wasn't trying to impress anyone tonight, so I grabbed my wallet and headed out.

Where the fuck was that brothel again? I'd visited it last time we were here. Some of the Team guys refused to pay for sex—they'd rather cheat on their wives or girlfriends with unsuspecting coeds or stay on ship all night reading the Bible. Fuck that. I didn't have a wife, or a girlfriend. Some woman back home to screw around on me while I was off training or deployed nine months out of the year? No thanks. I'd tried that once—our ship hadn't even left the dock before she had another guy's cock in her mouth. Never again. At least I wasn't one of those guys slipping in and out of women's lives, filling them with empty promises. I'd seen enough of those men growing up—assholes taking me to baseball games, vowing to be my new dad, fucking my mom and then vanishing. I never made any commitments—except to my country and to my men. Sleeping with a prostitute was the definition of safe sex to me.

Neon-colored buildings lined the streets, some marked with graffiti. A dark-skinned man with an AK-47 slung across his body approached me. "Hey Sailor, looking for a good time?"

Damn straight. I hadn't laid eyes on a woman in six months. I said no words, just nodded my head and followed him into an alley, where he frisked me for a weapon. I was all clear. The sun beat down on the broken pavement, and I realized what a dumbass I was for going to a brothel in daylight. But I didn't give a fuck.

The multi-colored beaded curtain crashed in the wind, and I heard some Caribbean music in the background. The man rang a bell, and at least a dozen women ran from the back of the ramshackle house. They were dressed in cheap heels and trashy nighties; this wasn't some high-class joint. But that was fine with me.

One brunette caught my eye. Her black thong was hiked high up on her hips, like she was stuck in some eighties music video. Light-skinned, long legs, small breasts. She seemed older and more withdrawn than the others—and she was the only one who didn't make eye contact with me.

I pointed. "Her."

The pimp let out a deep laugh. "Star? Good choice."

The other girls dispersed, probably grateful to get a small break from being forced to fuck a stranger.

But I didn't want to think about their pathetic lives. There was nothing I could do to improve their existences. My conscience was already filled with guilt—I didn't need to add their sob stories to my burden.

The whore led me down a hallway into a tiny room. The place reeked of cum and sweat, covered by some sort of coconut spritz. What did I expect for twenty dollars?

A tiny cot was pushed up to the left side of the room, a tattered teddy bear sat on the floor, and a plastic end table filled the other corner. Was this where she lived? There were a few needles lying haphazardly in the trashcan. Of course she was a heroin addict—how else could she live this life? I was a SEAL—I knew that these women were probably all forced into prostitution at a young age. They had once been little girls playing make believe, dreaming of princes and castles. But I was no prince. I'd done enough lifesaving in my time and I'd learned the hard way that I couldn't save them all.

"Star? What's your real name?" I didn't really care, but I felt that since she'd be sucking my dick, I should at least know her name.

She pursed her lips as if she was trying to say something but couldn't get the words out. Her face looked vaguely familiar, but I was certain I hadn't fucked her before. My last whore was Dominican: dark, curvy, black eyes. This chick seemed different, more tragic.

"Fine, we don't have to talk. Blow me." I took twenty dollars out of my pocket. If she did a good job, I'd give her a tip.

Over the years, I'd learned blowjobs were the best way to go with a whore. They always gave amazing ones, and I never felt guilty like I did when I took extra-long to come as I had with my ex-fiancée. I couldn't risk getting a nameless hooker pregnant and leaving a kid fatherless and growing up in this hellhole. Plus, there was less chance for a disease, especially since I always wore a condom. The Navy tested me every month so I figured there was minimal risk.

"Take your panties off."

Her panties dropped to the floor, revealing a nicely trimmed triangle. I loved it. Why did all those American bitches wax everything off? I was a man; I didn't want a little girl.

I sat on the edge of the cot. She knelt in front of me, unbuckled my belt, and glanced up at me, taking a moment to stare. She wore a rusty necklace with a small key charm. There were drug tracks on her forearms and a deep scar on her right shoulder.

Her eyes were hazel, deep set, and disturbed. I closed mine; I couldn't deal with her pain.

She rolled on the condom I'd handed her and took my cock in her mouth, slowly. I felt her warm tongue dance around me. Flicking, teasing, sucking. Damn, this bitch was good. Sometimes while getting a blowjob I couldn't help but imagine the whore was my girlfriend, or even my wife. That she loved me, was faithful to me, lived for pleasing me, and that having me take care of her even for just a few months out of the year was worth enduring the loneliness when I was gone. That she respected how I saw being a SEAL as more than a job—it was my calling.

I opened my eyes and placed my hand on the back of her head, her dark, wiry hair bobbing up and down. She stopped for a second, looked me dead in the eyes, and shifted from kneeling to sitting on her left side, exposing her right ankle. It had a tattoo of a surfboard painted with the American flag—why would a woman in the Caribbean have an American tattoo. Weird.

She got back down to business.

I didn't want to come, didn't want this moment to be over. But fuck, it had been so damn long. I mean, I barely even jerked off in my rack because my buddies were in the ones right next to mine.

Her mouth sucked on me hard, pulling and pushing. Man, why did this feel so good even with the latex barrier between us? I couldn't hold back any longer—I exploded into the condom.

She handed me a towel. I took off the condom, threw it in the trash, cleaned myself up and then pulled on my shorts. This part was awkward, always was. At least she hadn't spoken, so her voice wouldn't haunt my dreams or my conscience.

Her lashes blinked twice, as if she was deep in thought and wanted to tell me something. I didn't want to know her problems—I just wanted to get the fuck out of there.

I threw down five twenties and pushed myself off the cot. She stood up on her tiptoes, took my hand, and her lips grazed my ear, making sure to shield her hair over her mouth.

"My name is Annie Hamilton. I'm an American citizen. I was kidnapped on spring break five years ago. You're my last hope. Please save me."

What the fuck? This bitch wanted me to believe she was a sex-trafficked American? What kind of con was this heroin-addicted whore trying to pull on me?

"I gotta go." I shoved her off me. This was not my problem. She was not my problem. I walked out of that smelly room and didn't look back.

The streets of Aruba were bustling now in the early evening; tourists strolling through this idyllic Caribbean island, unaware that around the corner from where they were buying shot glasses and sundries, women were turning tricks for less than the price of their margaritas. The view of the beach was blocked by the endless taxicabs and the cobblestone streets were littered with cigarette butts.

Dammit. Of all the brothels, all the whores, why did I go there? Why did I choose her? I didn't need this shit. I headed to the closest bar to get drunk. Not one of those pretty tourist joints which served up fruity drinks. A seedy local dive, which offered nothing but hard liquor. No pictures of palm trees and beaches. The walls were barren, the air was thick with tobacco, and the bar stools had been cut with blades.

I should've listened to Kyle and fucked some college girl.

"Tequila, straight."

The bartender poured me a drink, then another. Smooth, sweet, salty, tart.

The more the liquor flowed, the more I tried to push her out of my mind. I thought about my dog back home, my mother, my ex-fiancée, my truck. I made small talk with the bartender; lied about my job, told him I was a tourist on a business retreat.

By the end of the night, I was blazed senseless. I stumbled back to the USS Ronald Reagan, our huge, naval nuclear-powered super carrier, and collapsed onto my rack.

There was one problem. Her voice. She had spoken with a perfect American accent; sounded like she was from California. And her vaguely familiar face now made me think I had seen her picture once in a magazine.

Christ. One fucking blowjob and now the whore was a constant presence in my brain. Maybe Kyle was right—I did need to get laid more often.

I closed my eyes and tried to sleep, praying to erase her from my memory.

2. Star

ANNIE HAMILTON. IN MY DRUG-FUELED haze, I took a chance. The words that I thought, that I knew I wouldn't have the strength to say overpowered my lips as if they had a mind of their own. I hadn't uttered my name in years. They'd given me a new one—Star—and a new identity—whore. Analía "Annie" Rose Hamilton—San Diego University's soccer star, Kappa Kappa Gamma sorority girl, and Bob and Linda's "perfect" daughter—was dead. Star—heroin addict and prostitute—was barely hanging on to life.

I hobbled over to the sink and brushed my teeth, scrubbing the bitter condom taste out of my mouth. My panties remained scrunched up on the floor, so I pulled them on and slumped back onto the cot. The bell would ring any second and I would have to line back up and greet the next group of men, or face a beating. I reached into my stash to get a quick fix.

What the fuck had I been thinking? For five years, I had lived this life, accepted my fate, and fought the urge to escape. I focused on survival, one day at a time, one man after the next. I knew my family was most certainly still looking for me, desperate to find answers as to what had happened to their princess the morning I had disappeared from the resort. I couldn't face them knowing what I had done to stay alive, who I had become. Would they accept me? Could I accept myself? And I didn't know if I would be able to live without the friend who had been there for me over the years. And that friend would never fit in at my parents' country club or with my sorority sisters. The friend that had held my hand through the beatings, the rapes. My only friend: heroin.

And I held a secret. A secret I would die for. The one light left in my life. And the truth behind my secret was yet another reason I doubted I would ever be accepted back into my former life.

The man who had just been in my room, in my mouth, he had been different. Different than the other men who'd haunted my doors, stuck their dicks inside me, penetrated my body and mind.

He'd asked my name—my *real* name. No one had ever done that.

That man was gorgeous—looked like he had just

walked off an action movie set. He wasn't just another American—no, that man had to be Special Forces. What if he was a Navy SEAL? Would he save me? I grew up in San Diego and would always see them training on the beach, running through the surf carrying logs and boats over their heads, when I was having brunch at the Hotel Del Coronado. They were a cult of masculinity: chiseled, wet and sandy. I could tell by his muscular body, his longer dirty, blond hair, and his scruffy beard. His attitude. He didn't try to make small talk or make me feel better about myself. He approached me like a job. A job he needed to accomplish. He was the kind of man who could save me. The kind who gave me hope that one day I could escape. And he picked me—I usually got chosen by old European businessmen and crooked Caribbean cops. My first thought when I saw him was maybe my parents had finally located me, and had sent someone to extract me. So, I took a chance. Knowing if my pimp found out I had opened my mouth for anything other than sucking cock, he'd kill me. I'd always thought that by age twenty-three, I'd be married to my college sweetheart, living in Encinitas with my dog and starting my career as a teacher. Maybe I'd be on my honeymoon in paradise, instead of turning tricks for tourists in hell.

I'd risked my life by revealing my identity. And he barely listened to me before he bolted.

I tied the rubber tube around my arm then

shoved the needle in my least-bruised vein. The warm, smooth fluid spiked through my body, soothing my soul. My pain stopped and I pretended I wasn't splayed on this filthy cot. Ten, twenty, thirty seconds of the most intense pleasure, warmth, and joy—the only release I had left in my life. I wrapped my arms around my body to contain my euphoria.

The bell rang. I leapt from the cot. Maybe he had returned? His eyes had given me a glimmer, a glint of warmth. I'd broken my own rules—I looked him in the eyes, I showed him my tattoo and my scar. I did my best to please him, imagined when I was servicing him that he was my boyfriend.

The girlfriend experience.

I'd never done that—I don't even remember what it's like to be turned on by a man. And I highly doubted I would ever enjoy sex again—even if I somehow managed to escape from this nightmare.

I returned to the line. Two Middle Eastern men stood there, picking out their victims. One pointed at me. Fuck.

Why me? I'd already pretty much aged out. Men always went for the barely legal girls. My face was now weathered; my eyes were hollow. How could any man get turned on by fucking a corpse? I was a shadow of who I once was. My family wouldn't even recognize me now. I'm sure I'd be an embarrassment to them—what if they didn't even want me back?

He followed me back to my tiny room, but I could still sense that beautiful man's presence. At least he had asked my name.

This guy said something to me but I didn't understand him. My mom was Mexican-American so I grew up speaking Spanish, a skill that definitely helped me blend in with the other girls. Over the years, I'd learned the nasty words in most languages. As my high school French teacher said, you never knew when you'd have an opportunity to practice your foreign language skills. If she only knew.

He took off my clothes and threw me on the bed. I shoved a condom in his face and luckily for me, he didn't fight it. I lay back on the cot and closed my eyes, praying it would be over soon.

Each pump, each thrust, each moan, made my skin crawl. His rum-spiked breath blew hot on my neck. Finally, he collapsed on top of me, and I didn't even have the strength to push him off. After a few torturous minutes, he rolled off me, threw the money on the floor and walked out of the room.

This was my life. How many more men could I take? Once my pimp decided he no longer had use for me, I would be history. He would trade me to another brothel, another island. Or kill me.

No hero was going to sweep in and save me. I had to find a way out of here, back to my life, back to the United States. I was running out of time before Star wiped every piece of Annie away forever.

I knelt by the side of my bed and clasped my hands in prayer. I was Catholic but stopped praying years ago, after all my prayers went unanswered and I endured daily beatings, rapes, torture, and drugging. But this time I wasn't praying to Mary, the Saints, God, or the Holy Spirit, the Trinity. I was praying to the man with the deep blue eyes and shaggy blond hair. I prayed he was the man I thought he was. I prayed he was capable of what I thought he was. I prayed he would believe me. I prayed he would return and bust me out of this hellhole so I could discover if life was worth living again.

3. Patrick

I ROLLED OUT OF MY rack the next morning and hit the head to take a piss. A hot shower would've been nice, but I had something more important to do.

I poured myself a cup of coffee, black, and went over to our computer and typed in the name she had given me. Annie Hamilton.

The screen lit up—articles, news clips, videos, websites. "American Analía 'Annie' Rose Hamilton Vanishes on Spring Break." There was even a wiki: "The Disappearance of Analía Rose Hamilton."

Could the drug-addicted prostitute from last night really be America's missing sweetheart? Maybe she was part of some elaborate con job? A light-skinned prostitute could've faked the American accent, learned the story, and used it to bilk johns like me out of cash.

I clicked on the first image—the cover of *People Magazine*. "Vanished without a Trace: Annie Hamilton." Those deep hazel eyes from last night stared back at me.

Fuck.

Those eyes were about the only part of her, which resembled the girl from last night. She was hardened, despondent, and scared. Those pretty eyes were now encased by dark circles, and had only given a dead stare.

I skimmed the first line; five years ago, just as she'd said. And by all accounts, she was still missing.

After five years, surely she was dead. Yet no trace of her body had ever been found. I remembered hearing about her disappearance, but I was deployed in Iraq at the time so I never knew all the details.

I read the first article. Annie and her boyfriend, Chris Porter, had taken a spring break vacation to the Caribbean. They'd partied until around two a.m. in the nightclub at their resort and multiple guests saw them dancing together. By all accounts, they'd both been extremely intoxicated and a few guests recalled that Chris seemed to be jealous when Annie climbed up on stage to dance with a professional ballroom dancer from the resort. At two thirty a.m., her boyfriend's key card was used to enter their hotel room, and he swore she was with him. Chris stated the last time he saw her was around five a.m. sitting on the balcony of their suite the morning she went missing. He figured she wanted to get fresh air and watch the sunrise, so he went back to sleep. A few other guests claimed they saw her around six a.m. in the elevator with the dancer. Chris passed a lie detector test and repeatedly insisted on his innocence. The dancer was also questioned but there wasn't any evidence to hold him. Authorities believed she'd committed suicide, or was killed by her boyfriend after a fight. Despite a FBI search The FBI had conducted a thorough search of the resort and the nearby ocean but no trace of her had ever been found.

Suicide? Doubtful. She was young, hot, in college and in love. Came from money. I guess she could've been depressed, but I figured it was a long shot.

As for the boyfriend? I felt bad for the guy. He was a pretty-boy, wealthy surfer from La Jolla who had probably never worked a day in his life. Tan and blond, he looked like one of those guys who sat on the beach smoking weed, laughing at the BUD/S candidates while they were running around carrying logs over their heads during Hell Week. Came from a good family, played water polo at San Diego University. He seemed normal enough, but how did anyone really know how he treated Annie behind closed doors? Maybe he abused her. If he killed her, then he got away with the perfect crime.

If he was innocent, his life was ruined from the suspicion and the guilt he must've felt not knowing what had happened to her.

I gazed across the ocean from my porthole. The resort was only a mile away. If she had been killed, surely there would've been some evidence—blood, clothes, a body. It didn't add up.

In the weeks, months, and years, which had followed, there'd been a few sightings of Annie on Aruba and on other neighboring Caribbean islands, but nothing ever panned out. Her family had even reportedly hired a former SEAL to find her, but he turned out to be a fraud.

I fucking hated any motherfucker who lied about being a SEAL. It was easy to figure these assholes out—just ask them their SEAL training class number. Not knowing your SEAL training class number is like not knowing your last name.

I still wasn't convinced yet that the prostitute was who she said she was. I didn't want to stake my career on a maybe.

I studied a few more websites. Her parents had created www.findannie.com.

There were childhood photos, lists of sightings, news articles, and links to television programs.

There was a letter begging for her return posted from Chris with pictures of the happy couple.

Then a photo caught my eye.

The tattoo on her ankle.

That surfboard with an American flag. So that's why she made sure I saw it. Just in case I was the man she thought I was.

The words of the Navy SEAL Code, our warrior creed, echoed in my head.

In times of war or uncertainty, there is a special breed of warrior ready to answer our Nation's call.

A common man with uncommon desire to succeed.

Forged by adversity, he stands alongside America's finest special operations forces to serve his country, the American people, and protect their way of life.

I am that man.

Fuck.

But tattoos can be faked. I needed more.

I clicked on another picture.

Yup—the scar on her shoulder. She'd shown me that also.

My heart beat rapidly in my chest, my jaw clenched.

I needed to see her face again, look into her eyes. That's the only way I'd know for certain.

Why hadn't anyone rescued her? She was an American for Christ's sake!

But this wasn't a fucking movie. There weren't FBI and CIA agents on the ground in Aruba searching for kidnapped Americans, especially since there was no proof she had been abducted. Any sightings of her would first be passed to the local police, who were corrupt as fuck. Her parents could've hired one of the many private contractor groups filled with former SEALs who did this shit for a living.

She didn't need a private contractor group—she now had me. I'd trained my entire adult life for missions like this one.

There was a three hundred thousand dollar reward for her safe return. But I didn't want any money. Giving Annie her life back would be reward enough. If I saved her, I had to remain anonymous. Any hint of an active duty Navy SEAL going rogue would ruin my career on the Teams.

I glanced back at her pictures. Man, she'd been beautiful. Could've been my high school sweetheart. She was half Latina, looked almost like a young Wonder Woman. Her black hair had been shiny; her hazel eyes had been bright. A soccer star, a prom queen, a little girl in pigtails. And I had treated her like she was a piece of trash.

Fucking traffickers. Most Americans were completely oblivious to the sex trade. They thought it only happened in third world countries. But girls were kidnapped off the streets in Middle America, and forced to service assholes like me. I wanted her to be just another piece of ass who I could use and forget, but the pain in her eyes reminded me too much of my own hell.

We were headed back to the states tonight. What the fuck was I going to do? Tell my men? Ask my command? It wasn't that easy. Everyone thinks Navy SEALs are above the law, that we can do whatever we please without any consequences. Like the ridiculous story about one of our snipers who shot and killed two civilian men and wasn't even brought in for police questioning. Bullshit. There's protocol, and busting into brothels was way out of our jurisdiction. I'd have to talk to my commanding officer. He'd send me to Captain's Mast for going to a brothel. Any authorized rescue attempt would have to be cleared with the FBI and CIA. There would be an investigation to see if she was who she said she was. They might set up a sting operation. And the crooked cops in Aruba could tip off her pimp. If her pimp had any inkling of what was going on, he'd probably kill her without a second thought.

I wasn't going to let that happen.

Were all those prostitutes trafficked? Prostitution was legal here, and I deluded myself to think that at least the women were there willingly. And I couldn't save everyone in the place. It would cause an international incident; most of them were probably from Eastern Europe or Central and South America. But I'd be damned if I let Annie, or any other American trapped there, spend one more day than they had to in that hellhole. Other men didn't get why I hadn't shed a tear when I found out my ex-fiancée had cheated on me. But the national anthem? "The Star Spangled Banner" had me bawling like someone shot my dog. I'd watched my buddies die protecting our country's freedoms. And I'd lay down my own life before I let some traffickers steal Annie's.

She was twenty-three now, two years younger than me. She'd spent her entire adult life in a foreign country as a sex slave. I couldn't even fathom her miserable existence.

My loyalty to Country and Team is beyond reproach. I humbly serve as a guardian to my fellow Americans always ready to defend those who are unable to defend themselves.

Enough men had used her and then abandoned her. I wasn't going to be one of them.

Vic made his way through the tangled maze of hungover SEALs in our sleeping quarters. "Want to get lunch?"

If I flaked on them two days in a row, they'd know I was up to something. "I can't. I'm going to get a massage."

Kyle's head popped up in his rack. "As long as it includes a happy ending, I'm in."

These men were my best friends—I didn't want to lie to them. We'd saved each other's lives more times than I cared to remember.

"No can do, I'm already late. I'll be back in a bit and we'll go have a drink before our ship leaves." I slipped a watch on my wrist and left the ship.

I had to see Annie before they shuffled her to another brothel and I lost the opportunity forever. Tattoos and scars could be faked. I needed to be one hundred percent certain the girl with the hollow eyes really was Annie.

Would the pimp get suspicious if I came back two days in a row? I doubted it. If she had survived five years, she must've gained their trust. They probably thought she was so strung out that she wanted dope more than she wanted her old life back. That's how these lowlifes worked—strip these girls of their identities and leave them with nothing left to fight for.

But she'd told me her name. She trusted me. And I'd walked away from her.

Some hero.

The streets seemed less bright today. I'd actually looked forward to my Team's mission in the Caribbean waters. Aruba was a better destination than Afghanistan as far as I was concerned. But now I'd rather be roasting in the mountains than investigating the underbelly of paradise.

I stopped by a tourist shop. Purchased some water, snacks, lotion, and a dress for Annie. Also bought her a small necklace, which I placed in my pocket.

The same pimp found me on the street. "Hey, hey. You had good time? Welcome back, my friend."

I hated the way these vipers called me friend. Did he even know that Annie was a kidnapped American? Often these girls were traded to other pimps, so he might not know her true identity if she kept her cover. Even though he had a gun, I could take this fool in a second, even unarmed. Were there more armed men watching this place? Without my men and my weapons, I couldn't take any chance of smuggling Annie out.

I followed him back to the brothel. He was about to ring the bell but I stopped him. "I want the same girl I had last night."

"Star? Sure, sure. How about two girls? I give you a good price."

I shook my head. "Nope, one will do. 'Star' did a good job."

"What's in the bag?"

I opened it up. "Some food, water, clothes, lotion. I wanted her to dress up for me and smell good. How much for an extra hour? I'm heading back out to sea tonight."

He rummaged through the bag, and then squinted his eyes. "I give her to you for two hours free, for your watch."

I didn't hesitate to hand it over to him.

His face broke out into a smile. He motioned to me and led me down the hallway, to her door. Then he turned and left, probably to lure the next jerk like me inside.

I paused before I opened the door. There was no going back; I needed to know one way or another if the woman behind this door was Annie Hamilton.

4. Star

MY DOOR SQUEAKED. HAD I missed the bell? I was crashing down so hard that the only rings I'd heard were in my mind. Jose would beat me if I missed line up and then he wouldn't give me any more dope tomorrow. It was still working hours, and I wouldn't have a break until well past midnight.

I glanced up from my bed, thinking it was one of the younger girls or maybe even Jose.

But it wasn't Jose. Or another girl. Or another client.

It was that man.

The bearded man from the other night stood at the door: chest erect, shoulders back, confident, strong, and sexy.

Was he here for another round?

Before I could say a word, he shut the door and

put his hand over my mouth. His deep blue eyes darted around the walls, probably scanning to see if there was a camera. He wrinkled his face when his glare hovered over the needles in the trashcan. The stench of my dope wafted through my drug den.

My chin dropped. I'm sure he saw me as nothing more than a heroin-addicted whore. I cowered, embarrassed about who I had become.

He turned his attention back to me. Without saying a word, he knelt beside me and grabbed my ankle, tracing his fingers over my tattoo.

He'd noticed. And my parents had actually once said to me I'd regret getting that tattoo one day. Little had they known this American surfboard might possibly save my life.

He sat on the bed and spoke in a low tone. "Annie, my name is Patrick Walsh—I'm a Navy SEAL. Sorry for running out of here the other night."

Holy fuck! I was right. He was a SEAL. He'd come back to rescue me.

I gasped. Was I still high? Was this a dream?

My body trembled. I wanted to scream, to cry, to kiss him, but I remained frozen.

"I'm sorry I didn't believe you."

But he did believe me. He'd come back; no one had ever come back for me. Over the years, a few tourists gave me knowing glances, as if they might have recognized me. One fat American businessman spent so much time staring at my tattoo, I'd been convinced he was going to report seeing me, but that had been over two years ago. This other American, who I'd thought was former military, acted so strange I'd been convinced he'd been sent to save me. But I'd never had the courage to utter my name to any client until the other night.

"Why don't you start by telling me what happened." He placed his strong hand on my knee, trying to comfort me.

In an alternate reality, I'd be so wet right now. Fucking a fine-ass Navy SEAL had once been my fantasy. Back in San Diego, I would've dropped my panties so fast for this man, begged for him to dominate me, screw me senseless.

These days, being touched revolted me, but his hand was different. Rough and blistered, yet firm and calming.

My lips parted and despite his warm skin, chills radiated through my body. For years, my hope had died. No fairytale ending was in store for me.

I tried to speak but I had lost my voice. Before I could tell him my sob story, tears stained my cheeks. I didn't want to come down from this high, and for once I wasn't talking about heroin, I was talking about the high of hope.

Could this man be my hero? The one who could finally break me free and give me back the life that was stolen from me?

The only thing I could imagine worse than the hell I had endured was to think, even for a second, that I had a chance of getting my life back. A chance to be whole again. And having nothing come of it. I wanted to enjoy this moment, this fantasy. Even if it only lasted one night.

5. Patrick

One look back into her hazel eyes and my doubts melted away. After five years, extensive manhunts, and expensive private investigators, I was the one who stumbled upon the long lost Annie Hamilton.

This time, she wasn't wearing sexy lingerie, probably because she hadn't been called out to the line. She was clad in a stained white tee shirt and pink cotton panties.

I debated apologizing for paying her to give me a blowjob. As much as I felt like a jackass for hiring a captive sex slave, deep down I didn't regret it. Probably from growing up listening to all of my mom's new age bullshit, but I believed everything happened for a reason. I'd found her. That was all that mattered.

Annie sobbed quietly. I could handle that. Being

raised by a single mom, I'd comforted her so many times growing up, it was as if I were the parent. Every time she had her heart broken, she lost a job, or she didn't have enough money for Christmas presents, I was the one who reassured her everything would be okay.

"Hey, hey, it's okay. I'm going to take care of you." I embraced her, her tiny frame almost disappearing in my strong arms. She buried her head into my chest. I would do anything to protect her—she'd been through hell and back and if she needed me to hold her, wipe away her tears, and tell her everything was okay, I would do that. I wanted to comfort her as much as I could. "You can relax. I'm not going to have sex with you, or make you touch me—that's not why I'm here." I had a thousand questions to ask her, but I didn't know how to start. She didn't release me, and just softly sobbed in my arms. When was the last time someone just held her and told her it was okay? The seconds turned into minutes and I didn't have the heart to let her go. How was I going to walk out of this room in two hours and leave her behind?

Finally, after what seemed like an eternity, she released me. I brushed back the hair on her face and handed her the paper bag. "I picked you up some things, clothes and stuff."

Mascara ran down her face. She opened the bag and took out a sundress, fresh panties and a bra, and some vanilla-scented lotion. I kept the necklace in my pocket.

Her tongue poked in her cheek and she swallowed.

"You can put the dress on if you want."

She nodded, stood up, and turned away from me as she undressed. Her sudden shyness surprised me, as less than twenty-four hours ago she had my dick in her mouth. I forced myself to not stare at her, and focused my glare on my feet and not her ass. A dull pain heaved in my chest. I hated myself for adding to her nightmare. At least I came back to do the right thing.

I needed to figure out the daily routine at the brothel; how far gone she was on heroin, and try to make a plan. There was no Intel team on the ground making action plans for me. I was in charge. And alone. No one to watch my back...or hers.

Ready to Lead, Ready to Follow, Never Quit.

There wasn't even an embassy in Aruba—the closest one was in Curaçao so even if I could somehow smuggle her out of here, she'd have nowhere to go. I needed to get her out of here and safely back on American soil as soon as possible.

Maybe I should've told Vic. But Vic played by the rules. He would've never let me go rogue. Or accompany me to a brothel, for that matter. Vic was a good man, a deeply pious Catholic. When his wife cheated on him during our last mission, I didn't know if he would make it. He spent every minute he could back in the States with his daughter, Carina. I knew he missed her like crazy. I couldn't imagine having a child. My dad left before I was born, so I wouldn't have a fucking clue about how to be a father.

Annie turned back toward me, dressed in her sweet yellow sundress, her hands fidgeting, as if she wanted approval.

"That looks nice on you," I offered, careful not to compliment her body. Though she was way too skinny, and her skin was speckled with bruises and welts, she was still sexy as hell. Her pouty lips curved up, her wild hair framed her face. My mind flashed and I wondered if the situation was different, if she was my girl, what it would feel like to hike up her sundress, rip off her panties and feel her wet pussy clench around me. I knew I could never again cross the line with her. From now on, she was nothing more than a mission to me.

She sat on the cot next to me. I wanted to move over and put an invisible line of distance between us, but I kept her close by my side.

I whispered into her ear, "I need to take a few pictures, okay?"

She shrugged and I took out my phone. Took a shot of her ankle, her scar, and her face.

"What happened, Annie? Tell me everything."

She remained silent, her dilated pupils fixed on the wall.

I pulled her to me and stroked her hair. "I'm sure they think by now they've broken you so much you'd never consider running. You can trust me. But I can only help you if you let me."

Her shoulders dropped and she blinked rapidly.

I didn't want to talk about myself, but I guess she needed more from me in order to open up. "I believe you, Annie." Every time I said her name, more tears welled in her eyes. "I saw your tattoo, your eyes, and your scar. I've read the news reports. Once I heard you speak, I knew you were an American, but I was spooked. I don't run away from problems, I fix them. If anyone can save you, I can. But if I told my command I found you, I'd have to go to Captain's Mast for going to a brothel. My career would be over, and then I'd never be able to get you out of here. And they would have to clear any rescue plans through the CIA and FBI, which could take months. The closest embassy is in Curaçao. I'm confident I can rescue you, I just need some more info. So please, help me help you."

She still didn't say a word.

I ran my hands over the scabs on her arms, her skin was clammy. "So, you shoot heroin?"

Her voice trembled. "Yeah. I can't stop. I want to, but they keep us high."

Right. Can't say I blamed her. "I get it. How long have you been in this brothel?"

"Don't know. I've been traded around." Every word she spoke I had to earn. The edge in her voice gutted me. "Different islands. Curaçao, Columbia, Venezuela. I speak Spanish so I don't stand out. I'm so fucked up, it's all a blur."

So that's how she'd survived so long. Her exotic looks and language skills must've helped her blend in with the other girls. "Are there any other American girls here?"

"No," she whispered. "There was a girl, Nicole."

Nicole Race? She'd disappeared on a family vacation a few years ago—I saw her name when I was researching Annie. She was last seen talking to a bartender at a popular tourist club in Curaçao. Was finding these girls not a priority? Didn't the FBI and CIA have Intel out here? "Where is she?"

"Dead." Her head shook a bit. "She OD'd. I'd convinced her we were going to be saved, but I'd been wrong. She gave up hope."

My breath shortened, the sense of urgency mounted. I needed to get Annie out of here before she succumbed to her addiction, or a fate even worse than her current life.

Annie brushed against my arm. I didn't want to touch her any more than necessary to comfort her. Enough men over the years had fondled her. "Who kidnapped you?"

"Renzo, the ballroom dancer at the resort. It was my fault. I left our room to go to the beach alone to take pictures of the sunrise and he grabbed me in the elevator."

Motherfucker. My blood burned. But I needed to focus on the future, not the past. "Annie, this isn't your fault. None of this is. I hope you know that. Are you ever allowed outside the brothel?"

"No." The little bit of color she had in her cheeks seemed to fade away.

"Why'd you tell me your name?"

She stopped shaking and touched my face, tracing my beard with her fingers. A spike of warmth radiated through me. "Because you asked me my real name. No one has ever asked me. I knew you were an American. I was praying you were a Navy SEAL." She paused and her fingers made their way down to my neck, my arms. "Your full beard, your strong arms, your muscles, your long hair—I knew you weren't some typical sailor. Something about your eyes . . . sounds crazy, but I trusted you. Despite the fact you'd just paid a hooker to give you a blowjob, I could tell you were a good man. I've seen so many men and their eyes were dark, cold. Or worse, dead. But yours . . . I can't explain it. They're kind, but hurt. For five years, I've held on to this fantasy that I'd be rescued. I prayed for you, I've dreamt of you. I knew you were sent for me. You are my only hope."

Whoa. Was she for real? I'm supposed to believe she willed me to save her, like some divine prophecy? I swallowed hard. She was probably flattering me to ensure I would help her, make me feel like I wasn't such a loser for hiring a hooker. I didn't need compliments; I'd save her no matter what.

This was getting intense. But I liked intense.

The courage it must've taken for this shell of a woman to open her mouth, say her name when she had no hope, showed me what a survivor she was. She was strong, like me.

"You told the right man. And I'm glad you showed me your tattoo. Your parents have it plastered all over their website."

Her lip curled. "I wasn't sure it was my ankle which had your attention at that moment. I figured if I did a good job," she went on, "then maybe you would believe me."

That made me feel like a grade-A asshole. My pants became tighter and I decided to change the subject.

"Do you have any questions for me?"

Her head bobbed forward, her eyes shifted. Maybe she just got high. I hadn't spent any time around drug addicts, so I didn't know what to expect. "What does everyone think happened to me?"

I didn't want to sugar coat it—she deserved the truth. "You committed suicide, Chris murdered you, or you ran away and started a new life. Chris has made several statements where he insists you were kidnapped, but most people believe he was trying to shift the blame off of himself."

Her head cocked up, and her left hand tugged at her earlobe. I could see the quiet intensity that she'd had with me snap. "Killed myself? Why the fuck would I kill myself? I had the best life—I was in college, had a great boyfriend, and was the star of my college's soccer team. I was drunk, yeah, but we were on land. Didn't anyone else see me that morning? Who the fuck thought Chris could've killed me? That's fucking ridiculous—he's a Buddhist vegan surfer, I mean the dude doesn't even eat dairy. Haven't there been sightings of me? I've been fucked by hundreds of men, even diplomats, police, FBI, secret service, military. Not one of those assholes reported me? Renzo took pictures of me and put them on a fucking escort website. He even covered my tattoo with a sheet. No one saw those? My dad is loaded—hasn't he sent people to find me? Or at least my body? He's just accepted that I'm dead?"

I rubbed her back. I wished I could take away all her pain. "I only know what I read today on the internet, but you're right, it makes no sense. Your parents hired some guy to find you, but he was a con man. There were some sightings but they couldn't be confirmed. I'm so sorry. I'm going to take care of you. You aren't alone anymore."

But she was alone. I knew damn well I was leaving to head back to the States tonight, without her. I'd racked my brain on every way I could get her out of here and safely to the embassy or to my ship. I was unarmed, unable to bring my weapons off the ship. There wasn't even an embassy in Aruba. A sloppy rescue attempt would get us killed. Even if I had told Vic and Kyle, there was nothing we could do to extract her tonight. Nothing.

Her breathing slowed down and she looked up at me, her eyes hopeful. Fuck, she felt her freedom was mere hours away. I couldn't tell her, not yet.

"Why'd you choose me? The other girls are younger, sexier. Why me?"

"No they aren't, not to me. You're beautiful, Annie. You were the only one I wanted." Defending my attraction to her, now knowing that she was a sex slave churned my stomach. "Look, I had no idea you were trafficked. Prostitution is legal here. I guess I wanted to believe this job was your choice. I'm not going to lie and say I've never been to a brothel. My life and job are stressful. I've been deployed for six months. I don't have a girl back home waiting for me. I'm not a cheater. For what it's worth, I'm sorry. I'm going to make it up to you, I promise."

She turned to comfort me, placing her hand on my back. "It's okay. I understand. You were just lonely."

A longing crept up inside me. I'd never admit it, but I was lonely. My men were more than coworkers, they were family. We were the most elite fighting force in the world, and supposed to be tough. But every now and then, I missed the closeness of being in a relationship with a woman.

Someone who worried about me while I was away, dreamt of me at night. Someone who was actually in love with me, not just the idea of being fucked by a SEAL. I couldn't offer a lavish lifestyle on my salary or daily attention because I was never around. Even so, I wanted to be the reason someone smiled in the morning.

Back to work. "How many men secure this place?"

"Jose. And Renzo. And others. They know everybody. I don't think you can save me."

"I've taken men a thousand times more dangerous than them. Annie, I'm going to get you out of here, but I can't do it today. I'm deployed and our ship leaves in a few hours." Her head started shaking, but I continued. "I need my weapons, to case the entire building, the surrounding area, get a car, and find a safe house for you. Bring a few of my buddies. You have to act normal. Do what they say. We're leave Aruba tonight to return home, but I will come back for you, I promise."

She pulled a fistful of her hair and rocked her head back on the cot. "No, please don't leave me here. You found me. You said you could save me. You came back! Come back and save me tonight! I'll be ready. I know you can." She rubbed her skin.

Hell if I was just going to lie there and watch her rock herself back and forth, like she was in some mental institute. She needed someone to comfort her, hold her, and tell her that her nightmare would be over soon. I took her in my arms and flipped her on top of me. She nestled her head on my chest. "I won't let you down, Annie. I will get you out of here and back to your family. I would do anything to save you today, but I can't. I promise you I'll spend every moment figuring how to get you back to your family."

She let out a pained breath. "Please, Patrick. Please, take me tonight. I need to go home. You don't understand. We have to get out. I'm going to die here. I can't take another day in this life. I'll do anything you ask."

She attempted to kiss my neck, but I pulled away and sat up, holding her to my side.

"I have to leave. But I have something for you." I rummaged through my pocket and retrieved the necklace, and placed it around her neck.

She gasped as if it was expensive jewelry, not a cheap fake gold chain with an anchor charm. I hoped if her pimps figured it had no value, she'd be more likely to be allowed to keep it.

I stroked her forehead. "Every time you look at it, know that I'm working on extracting you. You aren't invisible—you're invincible. I know you're alive. I know your name. You've survived this long and I will get you out of here." My pulse raced and I was disgusted with myself for being attracted to her in her present state. Her vulnerability was like a sword in the chest and a shot to my dick. I wanted to both protect her and fuck her and it was a combination, which could get both of us killed.

Her voice cracked. "Please, take me. You said yourself you have a few hours 'til you leave. Just go get your guns and buddies and save me. I'll do anything." Her hand reached in between my legs and she stroked my cock over my jeans. "Don't leave me here. I shouldn't be here. You don't understand. It's not just—"

I firmly moved her hands off my pants. "Don't, Annie. You don't ever have to touch me again. You don't owe me anything—saving you is my only mission now. I'm sorry, but I have to go."

"Patrick!" She started looking desperate, clutching me now. "Promise me you'll tell Chris I didn't kill myself. And my parents that I love them."

"You'll be able to say whatever you want to your boyfriend and your parents yourself. Soon." I never made promises I couldn't keep. And if I couldn't save Annie, if she died and I couldn't get her home safely, I'd never be able to forgive myself.

Her body was shaking. "What if I'm not here when you come back? What if they trade me?"

Fuck it. My hands clutched her body in a tight embrace. I wished she could read my mind and trust that once I committed to something, nothing would come in the way of achieving my goal. "I will find you. No matter what."

My word is my bond.

I pushed her off me, and rolled off the cot. I

pressed one hundred dollars into her hand, opened the door, then walked out of her room, and out of the brothel. Staying any longer would arouse suspicion, and I couldn't fuck this up for Annie.

Every step I took away from her tore me up inside. Why should I be safe when she was stuck here turning tricks? Hadn't she been through enough hell for a lifetime? I should've knocked out her pimp and carried Annie to safety. But a hasty plan like that could get us both killed. I needed to be patient to ensure the success of my mission.

I stand ready to bring the full spectrum of combat power to bear in order to achieve my mission and the goals established by my country.

6. Patrick

I PACED AROUND THE LIVING quarters of our ship as we set sail back to San Diego. I couldn't focus on anything except saving Annie.

I pulled Vic and Kyle into an empty rec room away from the rest of our Team.

Vic sat down in a chair. "Dude, what's going on with you?"

I stared at the drab gray walls, hesitating to tell them.

Kyle glared at me. "Spill it, Walsh." Kyle was a complete badass. He was one of only a handful of African-American men on the Teams, and unlike Vic and me, he was an officer. He'd been a linebacker in the NFL, and had been recruited through a joint partnership with the NFL and the Navy Special Warfare programs. Kyle gave up all that fame and money to join the Teams. There was a saying once on our recruiting posters, something like, "*He'll never win MVP, never get a Super Bowl ring—some heroes don't play games.*" Kyle was the living embodiment of that quote.

I didn't want to speak. So I logged into the common computer and pulled up a website on Annie.

Kyle focused on the screen. "Yeah, Annie Hamilton. Everyone knows about her. Fine as fuck. Got drunk and vanished from a resort out here. I bet her stoner boyfriend killed her. What's your point?"

I took a deep breath. "She gave me a blowjob last night at a brothel."

Kyle laughed. "Sure she did."

Vic shook his head at me, probably not sure whether or not I was joking. "Fuck you, man. She's someone's daughter. That's not funny."

"I'm not laughing. I didn't want to believe it either. She was fucking kidnapped and forced into sex slavery. I went to a brothel last night and this chick gave me head. Afterwards, she said her name was Annie Hamilton. I thought she was trying to con me, but it's fucking her: hazel eyes, Californian accent. And she made a point to show me her shoulder scar and ankle tattoo. Here, look at the pics." I handed Kyle my phone and he scrolled through the pictures while Vic looked on.

"I went back today to be one hundred percent sure. I'd fucking bet my Budweiser on it."

The room fell silent. We didn't joke about "The Budweiser," our trident, our Navy Insignia. It was pinned on every Navy SEAL, after completing the BUD/S training,

My Trident is a symbol of honor and heritage. Bestowed upon me by the heroes that have gone before, it embodies the trust of those I have sworn to protect. By wearing the Trident I accept the responsibility of my chosen profession and way of life. It is a privilege that I must earn every day.

Kyle put his hand on my shoulder. "You're serious. You fucking think you found Annie Hamilton in a Aruban whorehouse?"

"She's pretty wrecked, but she's alive. A heroin junkie barely holding on. It's a miracle she's survived these last five years. Now, how are we going to get her out?"

Vic shook his head. "You fucked a hooker? That's low, even for you, Walsh. Go tell Captain Marshall. You realize you're going to get charged for solicitation."

"Shut your fucking cock holster. Who the fuck do you think you are telling me what to do? You're not my sea daddy. Of course I know I can get charged, but I don't give a shit. We need to save her. We're fucking SEALs. No one else is going to do it. Don't you see? I was meant to be on this deployment, this SEAL Team. To rescue her. But we aren't going to tell Captain Marshall—or anyone else on the Team, for that matter. The Navy would have to go through the proper channels. It's too risky. There have been sightings of her before and no one did shit. I'm going to rescue her. You going to help me? Or you going to fucking rat my ass out?"

Kyle didn't hesitate. "I'm in."

Vic bit his lip. "So am I." I knew Vic would help, even though he liked to follow protocol.

Kyle put his hand on my back. "Yup. Not even worried. These dumbasses are jokes compared to the guys we usually deal with."

He was right. I'd been in firefights with the Taliban, overtaken Somali pirates, and offed members of drug cartels. A low-grade Caribbean white-slavery ring didn't scare me.

We train for war and fight to win.

We had two weeks at sea to come up with a plan before we arrived back in San Diego. The second my feet touched the ground on shore, I was going to hop on the next flight to Aruba. She'd survived five years. I'd never forgive myself if I couldn't bring her home to her family, home to the United States. What was the point of being called a hero if I couldn't save her? It didn't matter that rescuing her wasn't an official mission. She was my mission.

We expect to lead and be led. In the absence of orders I will take charge, lead my teammates and accomplish the mission. I lead by example in all situations.

7. Star

My mind raced. He wasn't coming back. He had left me. Another man who used and abandoned me, but even worse, he'd given me false hope. He knew I was whom I said I was, the hell I'd been through, and he had just left me here.

It had been more than two weeks. The longest weeks of my life—even longer than the first weeks I had gone missing. Back then, I had been slipping in and out of consciousness so I hadn't even been aware of my surroundings. I didn't know who or where I was, drugs shooting through my veins.

Why did he have to come back and give me hope? I didn't want to believe him, be let down again by another man. But what choice did I have?

I crept into the bathroom and turned on the shower. The lukewarm water beaded down my body, highlighting my scars. How much longer could I go on like this? I wondered what Patrick was doing at this precise moment. Was he thinking of me, planning my rescue? Or was he partying somewhere with his buddies, paying for another whore to service him? Why did I believe him? This was a man who paid for sex in a whorehouse. Sure, all men had needs, but I didn't know if I could ever respect a man who used a woman for sex, knowing she was a living corpse with no control over her body or life.

Patrick was nothing like the men I'd known before I was kidnapped. He was rugged, masculine, and unfiltered. My father was a proud and honorable man. He and my mom had been married for twenty-six years and he always treated her and me with such love and respect. He prided himself on having the perfect wife, the perfect daughter—how did I even fit into that picture anymore? I shuddered and it wasn't from the now ice-cold water. Thinking of the immense pain my father must be experiencing, unable to find his daughter, almost seemed worse than enduring my daily grind.

I'd had a boyfriend at the time I vanished. Chris was a marine biology major, and a world-class surfer. And Patrick said he'd been a suspect in my supposed murder? My careless decision to leave my room at dawn to take pictures ruined his life too. I'm sure he'd moved on now, not that I could blame him. Who would ever want me knowing I had been with hundreds of men? Even if I came back, I couldn't really see his parents accepting me into their family; a smack-addicted whore doesn't belong at the yacht club.

I scrubbed my body with the soap, until my skin was almost raw. Sometimes when I came down from a high, my skin burned and itched and I wanted to gouge it off my body. No matter how much I scoured and cleansed, I felt so dirty.

The steam filled the room and I exited the shower. Within an hour, I'd be back on the line, waiting for my next john.

I hated sex. Hated it. I could never learn to enjoy it again. It had even become more painful after Patrick had returned. Every time a man touched me, I wanted to vomit.

I'd give him a month or two. If he didn't come back for me, I needed to consider my options. Ha— back when I was younger, the word options to me meant travel, colleges, cars, jobs. Today, the only options I had available to me were to continue to live this miserable life, or to end it all. I couldn't go on like this forever.

But I had a reason to live. A reason to hope. And for now, that was enough to keep me going.

8. Patrick

KYLE, VIC AND I HEADED down to the ship gym to get one last workout in before we docked in San Diego. Tomorrow we were going to fly to Aruba. Adrenaline pumped through my veins yet I was able to control my emotions. I wanted to kill these motherfuckers, but to avoid an international incident they would have to do something really stupid for me to pop them off.

I was glad Kyle and Vic had my back. That's the thing with Team guys—we were more than brothers, we were bonded for life.

Kyle smacked me on the head. "Shit, man. I don't see why I can't get laid with one of the other whores first and then we can save your girlfriend. I'll be quick."

I hit him back. "Yeah, your ex mentioned your little problem. But sorry, not going to risk it. And she's not my girlfriend."

Vic shook his head, disgusted with us both. Kyle and I partied with the best of them, but poor Vic still hadn't learned his lesson after his ex-wife had cheated on him. He harbored some fucked-up fantasy that he'd find a girl to be faithful to him when he was away; some delusion that he might be able to have a marriage, which defied the Navy SEALs infamous eighty percent divorce rate. Optimistic bastard.

"Whatever you say, man." Vic laughed. "I know you. You've been obsessed with her since you met her. She's all you've talked about for the past two weeks. Once you save her, she'll worship you. You two will end up getting married. Mark my words. And she's from San Diego—how convenient. Plus, you said yourself, she gave great head. Sounds like a match made in Hell Week if you ask me."

"Fuck you, Vic. I'm not saving her because I love her. I don't even know her. I'm saving her because it's the right thing to do." But Vic's words resonated with me. Annie was all I thought about. Though I hadn't had more than a cheap sexual encounter and an awkward conversation with her, over the past weeks I'd learned everything I could about her. I'd watched childhood videos of her and her family from their website, seen interviews of her parents crying and begging for her safe return. She'd wanted to be a teacher and had volunteered with a dog rescue. And, though at first I saw her as just another woman who could satisfy me, now I couldn't wait to see her again. Even if it would be to watch her walk away in the end.

I could never make any woman happy. Especially not one who had been through so much and seen men at their worst. I doubted Annie would ever be able to trust a man again.

I loved women. All women. My mom taught me never to disrespect a woman. I'd given my heart to one once—I'd been faithful to her, encouraged her dreams, and supported her. Once, when I'd been deployed for six months, I arranged to have flowers delivered weekly to her house, with notes I'd written ahead of time and had given to the florist. And my ex gutted me. All the times I was stuck in some hole in Afghanistan, dreaming about her, she was screwing around on me. I didn't need that complication; my job was stressful enough. I needed my home life to be peaceful, because my line of work was anything but. The only men in the Teams who had successful marriages were married to women who were completely strong, honest, and loyal. Faithful women, who were both mothers and fathers to their children when their husbands were away. If I ever found a woman like that, I'd marry her in a heartbeat. It was impossible to build that type of relationship when I was never home. Since I'd turned eighteen, I'd spent most of the past seven years deployed or out training. In all that time, with the exception of BUD/S, I'd spent a grand total of eight months in San Diego, broken into two or three-week intervals. So I chose to be single until I retired, yet I was still a man and had my needs. It didn't help that I was plagued by the memory of Annie's mouth on my cock and her hands gripping my thighs as I came.

    I knew despite my best efforts, I'd worry about what would happen to Annie after I dropped her off at the embassy. I hoped she could heal and recover. But it wasn't my problem. She wasn't my problem. I would do my job and get her back to safety and then I had to get the fuck out of there. I'd seen what the media did to rediscovered treasures—they stalked them like celebrities. I could never be part of that media circus, not with my job, my life.

    I'd fulfill my duty to her and keep my promise. But after that, she was on her own. There was no other way. She had a family and a boyfriend waiting for her anyway. I could never fit into her life and she could never be a part of mine. She'd have to forget she ever met me, just like I hoped she would forget all the torture she endured. And I could go back to living my life the way I liked to.

    Alone.

9. Star

THE DOOR OPENED TO MY dimly lit cell. Had Patrick returned?

"Get up, princessa."

Jose stormed in.

Fuck.

"Get dressed, we're leaving."

My palms became moist and it wasn't because I was coming down. Had he somehow heard me tell Patrick my name? Years of building trust all thrown away in a careless moment.

"Why? Where are we going?"

Jose smirked, I recognized that look.

He was trading me.

Like Eva last month. One day, he came in the middle of the night and took her. And we never saw her again.

"Just put on your nice clothes. And your

makeup. We leave in ten."

"But what about my—"

"No more questions. It is taken care of."

No. I couldn't leave! Patrick could still come back for me. He was my only hope. The only way I could foresee reclaiming my life.

"Please, Jose." I batted my eyelashes. I would do what I had to. Sliding my hand up his thigh, I leaned into him.

He pushed my hand away. "Get ready."

I bit my lip. I never left the brothel. The pain of facing the outside world, seeing people who were enjoying their lives, even just a glimpse of my past, was more than I could handle.

"Don't worry about it. I'll find you."

But how could he? For the past five years, I'd been invisible. I was sure my father had hired private investigators to look for me. And what about the FBI? How could this SEAL locate me on his own if no one had been able to before?

My dress, a skin tight, tacky fuchsia number, the type of outfit I would've made fun of back at home, was now the highlight of my wardrobe. Black, plastic heels completed my ensemble. One pump of body spray and I was ready to go.

Would my new pimp torture me? I survived this horror too many times to count. At least here, I knew the routine. I had earned Jose's trust. He didn't rape me anymore and I had seniority amongst the girls. Who knew what hell waited for me somewhere else.

Jose arrived back at my door, wearing his crisp, white suit, a few of the other girls crowded around him. He only dressed up when he did a trade. "We go."

"We're all leaving?"

"Yes, we're moving to new house."

He let me take my purse, even though there wasn't much in there. Condom, gum, a hair clip, some lube. Should I take my smack? I couldn't live without it. I shuffled my feet across the concrete floor and followed him and the others outside.

The purple sunset was breathtaking. I remembered seeing this sunset the last night before I was taken. I was a spoiled bitch back then. Chris wanted a romantic vacation, but I wanted to let loose. Partying with the dancer in the club the night before I'd been taken was my right. No one could control me. Renzo later told me watching me dance on stage with the band made him determined to make me his. What a naïve fool I had been.

Jose shoved us into a van. I stared out the window, holding back sobs.

The driver started the engine, and I burst into tears.

"Hey honey, it's okay. We'll be fine," Sveta offered.

But she didn't know why I was crying. I'd told no one about Patrick. I'd done everything he'd asked of me, not aroused suspicion.

The van sped away, flashes of neon buildings whizzed by my eyes like a movie. I held my necklace. I didn't believe he would find me. I didn't believe in anything anymore. As the brothel disappeared in the distance, any hope I'd had of being rescued vanished with it.

10. Patrick

MAN, I WAS FUCKING TIRED. Thirteen hours by plane, including a redeye and a layover in Miami, and our airplane finally touched down at the Queen Beatrix airport, Aruba at sunrise. Had this been Annie's last sight before she had been taken? Her desire to photograph its beauty had cost Annie her freedom. Today, I would liberate her. I couldn't wait to see the look on her face once I'd saved her, hold her, and tell her she was free. All the training I'd gone through in my life had prepared me for this mission. The excitement, the adrenaline, and the high of completing a mission were indescribable. But liberating Annie would be the biggest reward of all.

Vic, Kyle, and I left the airport and headed to the private dock to stow our gear on our yacht rental.

We made our way through the maze of scuba

tours, glass bottom boats, and moonlit cruises. A middle-aged bearded guy with a ponytail and a beer belly met us at the dock, dangling the keys.

"You must be Dave." Kyle shook his hand, and Vic and I followed suit.

"Nice to meet you. *The Cleito* is all cleaned up and ready for you."

I glanced at Vic and Kyle. *The Cleito.* In Plato's myth of Atlantis, Cleito bore Poseidon ten sons. An obscure Navy SEAL trident reference, but we all understood the significance of the name instantly.

"And I secured you the weapons you wanted."

"We appreciate it." We couldn't bring our own weapons and check them on a commercial airplane.

Dave handed me the keys and narrowed his eyes toward me. "So, what are your plans? I know some great scuba spots."

I placed the keys in my pocket. "Thanks, man. Just wanted the guns in case we encounter any pirates. We're just going to relax, go fishing, and snorkel."

Dave glanced at our sea bags, which concealed our night-ops equipment. He was no dummy, a former old school Frogman. He probably sensed we were planning something other than checking out the local tropical fish. "Well, I'm happy to show you around. Anything you need." He placed his hand on my shoulder. "Please, don't hesitate to ask."

"We will." I eyed Kyle, who nodded toward me.

We could trust this man. Any BUD/S class, any trident. He was one of us. Basically fucking family.

"Well, let me give you a tour." He led us on the boat. It was no luxury yacht by any means, but it would suit our needs well. Downstairs there was a small galley, upstairs there were two cabins—one with two narrow bunks and one with a queen, a head, and a tiny living area. And a small area to relax up on the top deck. I gave Kyle the keys and he fiddled around with the controls.

We spent the rest of the day stocking up the ship with food, drinks, and supplies. I'd bought Annie clothes, shoes, toiletries, magazines, books, and a small duffle bag so she wouldn't have to go to the embassy empty handed. Wasn't sure what she was into, but I figured anything, which could keep her mind off drugs and what she'd been through would be a good bet. I hadn't a clue how long she'd be kept at the embassy, so I wanted to take care of her, even if I couldn't be there.

Hours later, the sun had finally set. We cleaned, loaded, and concealed our weapons.

We'd gone over the layout from the diagram I'd sketched when I returned from the brothel that night. We weren't too worried about smuggling her out. The plan was to head over to the brothel at night, posing as clients. Once I was inside the room with Annie, Kyle and Vic would take down the pimp until I smuggled her out of there. We weren't going to use force unless necessary.

We demand discipline. We expect innovation. The lives of my teammates and the success of our mission depend on me – my technical skill, tactical proficiency, and attention to detail. My training is never complete.

After we rescued her, we were going to take her to the embassy. The full plan should take us three days tops.

I was ready to give Annie her life back.

Kyle stood up. "Let's do this!"

Operation Rumpelstiltskin was ready to go down.

We'd all dressed casually. I had no fear—this was more like a training exercise than a mission.

Nothing could go wrong.

We walked through the back alleys of Aruba. A rush pulsed through my body. In less than an hour, Annie's nightmare would be over and a whole new world would begin.

Five blocks away—the cool night breeze blew across my face. I was so close to Annie, I could taste her. Knowing we were breathing the same air, and we were minutes away from seeing each other again sent tingles through my body.

Four blocks away—every step brought me closer to her. The town was unusually quiet; I could almost hear my heart beat in my chest.

Three blocks away—Kyle turned and nodded toward me. A silent confirmation that we would be successful. He had no doubts of our abilities, our plan.

Two blocks away—my palms sweaty. Something seemed off. Usually by the time I reached this street, I could already see her pimp scouting for johns. But the streets were hauntingly empty.

One block away—my chest clenched. A distant smell of smoke wafted through my nostrils. My breathing became labored.

When at last we turned onto the street, my jaw tightened. The brothel was nowhere in sight—instead, ashes were strewn across the ground, burnt mattresses collapsed in the street, a lone teddy bear tattered in the rubble.

It was gone—she was gone.

I'd failed her.

Vic put his arm around my shoulder. "You sure this is the place?"

"Positive."

Kyle sifted through the embers, eyes focused. "I'm sure she's alive and they just moved her. Buildings down in these parts have a way of mysteriously catching on fire."

Tears rimmed my eyelids and I could feel the pulse in my throat. I scooped up the teddy bear from the ground, remembering that it looked like the one I'd seen in Annie's room the first night I met her.

A man walked by wearing a watch which looked like the one I'd given the pimp.

I ran and shoved him against the next building.

"Where did you get that fucking watch?"

He quivered. My hands clasped his throat and he let out a croak.

"Where is she, you motherfucker? Where did you take her? Tell me before I fucking snap your neck!"

His hands flailed in the air. "I don't know—I don't know what you are talking about. A man sold me this watch."

He quivered, and once I got a closer look, I realized it wasn't my watch.

Vic and Kyle dashed after me, pulling me off the man.

I stood back. "Get the fuck out of here." He scurried down the street.

Vic stood in my personal space and made strong eye contact. "Pat, we'll find her."

I backed away from them, and started back into town.

If she were still alive, I would find her. Annie had survived this long. I prayed she wouldn't give up, because I would scour every corner of this Earth until I found her. Nothing would stop me. Not even my job—I'd fucking take extra leave from my Team.

I will never quit. I persevere and thrive on adversity.

11. Patrick

WE SAT AROUND IN THE yacht and hatched a plan over beer and pizza. I had less than four weeks to find her. Four weeks until our leave was over and we deployed to the Middle East for six months. By then she would be lost forever. And so would I. There was no more room for errors.

Kyle always tried to take charge. "It's easy. Let's go and ask around town until someone talks. Or we can ask Dave for help. He knows this area."

"It's not that easy." I took a swig of my beer and studied the breaking waves. "I don't want to involve Dave unless we have to. He's a local. We can't raise suspicion. They could kill her if the wrong person found out."

Vic nodded in agreement. "We contact the FBI, go through the channels. That's the best way."

Kyle and I exchanged a glance. I'd already informed Vic that telling the FBI wasn't an option. Especially now—I'd wasted enough time.

"I fucked up. I should've told you guys the night I met her. We could've gotten her the next night when I went back. Now it'll be on my shoulders if she ODs or winds up murdered in a ditch."

Kyle placed a reassuring hand on my back. "Don't beat yourself up about it. We had to get back on the ship that night. And we didn't have access to our weapons. What the fuck could we have done? Save her and then drop her off somewhere? And don't be such a fucking pussy. She didn't get moved because you came back. They move these girls all the fucking time."

I knew that, she'd even told me that. But I hadn't listened. Too cocky, and now I didn't have a fucking clue where she was.

I stood up. "Let's go."

I didn't have to explain myself. Vic and Kyle pounded back their beers, polished off their pizza, and we left.

We weaved in and out of the underbelly of Aruba. Must've hit up a dozen more brothels. It was so fucking depressing. I wanted to get hammered so I didn't have to deal with the guilt I felt for hiring Annie. How could I have ignored her suffering? Even if she hadn't been trafficked, I realized now that visiting any of these brothels was so wrong.

My mom would be disgusted with me. Some of the prostitutes couldn't have been older than fourteen. The older ones reeked of desperation. Dead eyes, bruised bodies, drugged minds.

There was no sign of Annie.

At all of these brothels, I never recognized any of the other girls who'd worked with Annie. I knew they couldn't have all just vanished into the night. They had to be somewhere.

At the next brothel, Kyle disappeared into one of the rooms with a girl. He said he was going to 'take one for the team' so we didn't arouse suspicions.

When he emerged from the room, he had a big smile on his face.

"Was she that good?" I asked.

"Wouldn't know. I couldn't bear to fuck her, in case she was another American sex slave. Just gave me a hand job. Not half bad but I do a better job myself. Anyway, I told her I had fucked this amazing whore at the brothel that had burnt down. She said she'd heard a bunch of girls were just moved to Curaçao." He smirked. "Told you I'd take one for the Team."

I pressed my palms downward on my pants; this time I didn't want to be overly confident. The cool Caribbean breeze calmed my mind. Annie had mentioned she'd been transferred to Curaçao once. Made sense that she might be back there now.

Curaçao was a mere island away.

Pictures of Annie in various situations raced

through my mind. Annie being raped by some sweaty fat ass with tentacle hands and bad breath. Annie shooting up and stoned out of her mind on the dirty floor of a dark room. Annie being beaten by an overenthusiastic pimp with a heavy hand and no one to protect her. Annie crying alone at night because she'd finally given up hope that I would find her.

Over the years, I'd participated in many missions. Accomplishing them gave me a great sense of pride for my country, but I'd never felt as connected to a mission as I did to this one. I was meant to be in the brothel that night, to choose her, to ask her name. Even my ex-fiancée cheating on me led me to that moment, that decision, because if she had been faithful, I would be married to her and would've never set foot in a brothel. I may have many character flaws, but cheating was not one of them.

As we made our way toward the dock, I breathed in the crisp island air. The stars illuminated the ocean. When was the last time "Star" saw stars? Maybe wherever she was, she had a small window with a glimpse into the night. I closed my eyes for a second and focused on her soul, willing her to feel my presence.

I am never out of the fight.

12. Patrick

MY EYES WERE GRITTY FROM lack of sleep and not even the black tar Kyle claimed was coffee could wipe the fog from my brain. A restless night on the piece of shit boat coupled with vivid nightmares of Annie's fate had me feeling edgy and irritable. I couldn't relax until we'd gotten this shit done.

With the boat safely docked in a slip, the three of us made our way through the energetic market, elbowing through hordes of tourists and locals hawking their wares. The sun was already baking a sea of bodies on the stretch of beach, and though I wore faded jeans and a frayed t-shirt with a cap pulled low over my eyes, I felt the heat heavy on my skin. Kyle bought a tacky floral shirt, his attempt to dress like a tourist and blend in. Vic followed at a distance, strolling leisurely from shop to shop along the beachfront road.

We'd rented a car and reserved a hotel room in the middle of town. Until we found her, we wanted to make sure we were staying in the center of the tourist hub so we could do our best to blend in with the throngs of visitors.

At night, Kyle, Vic, and I set out again, scouring the red lights. The ones in Curaçao seemed more upscale than the ones in Aruba. Most were set up like bars. Men could sit and order drinks at little tables and chat up the hookers. I guess that was great for the men who liked to pretend these women were actually interested in them, instead of admitting they were paying for sex. I preferred to be honest with my intentions so I never needed to play any games or delude myself any more than I already did.

After another long night of too many drinks and too bright neon lights, we'd come up empty-handed. No Annie.

Kyle convinced us to cool off at the hotel bar, Enrique & Richie's. It was dark and pulsed with loud music, heavy on the bass. Spring break was out in full force. Coeds writhed on the small dance floor with candy-colored drinks and short skirts paired with bikini tops. Most were already halfway to blitzed, and I couldn't help but wonder if one of them would be the next Annie.

The other American girl who went missing, Nicole Race, had last been seen at this bar.

Vic and Kyle hit on girls, but I was too fucking depressed to make small talk. I sat alone at a table in the corner, drinking whiskey. Why should I be out having fun in paradise, while Annie was still turning tricks in hell?

Think, motherfucker. What am I missing?

My mind drifted, and I zoned out listening to the Calypso music. The beat of the steel drums shook my shot glass.

Steel. Drums.

Annie had said the last thing she'd remembered the morning she had been taken was that the dancer entered her elevator. And she had said she knew Nicole before the poor girl had overdosed. This couldn't just be a coincidence.

I glanced over to the dancer and my eyes narrowed. A larger than life man with piercing dark eyes; he wore a pink shirt and danced to those drums as if he didn't have a care in the world, his arms wrapped around a blonde tourist. And he was wearing a watch. Was it mine?

I slammed my whiskey glass down, the liquid sloshed over the rim. I'd been wrong before back at the burnt down brothel. I needed to be certain.

Kyle was busily grinding some girl on the dance floor, so I approached Vic.

"I need to get out of here. Just going to take a walk."

Vic raised his eyebrow at me. He knew me well

enough to know something was up. "I'll go with you. Let me just pull Kyle away."

At this point, I had a loose hunch, a clenching in my gut. Ultimately this was my mission, my fight. I'd looked into Annie's eyes; I'd given her my word. Her freedom was my responsibility. "No man, I'm good. I kind of want to be alone. I'll meet you back at the room."

Vic nodded, patted me on the back. "Okay, bro."

I made my way to the alley near the back of the club. There was a van parked there. A crooked tree was painted on its side door. For once, luck was on my side. Our rental car was just up the street. I could watch from inside, and when the band and dancer left, I'd be ready to follow.

Hours passed. I was tired as fuck but didn't so much as close my eyes to risk sleep. Staying up casing this van was easy compared to the training I'd endured. In BUD/S Hell Week, I'd survived on only four hours of sleep in five and a half days. To this day, every time I was tired during a mission, I could hear my instructors' words echo in my head, taunting us, trying to get us to ring the bell three times and quit.

Anybody who quits right now gets hot coffee and doughnuts. Come on, who wants a doughnut? Who wants a little coffee?

There was no coffee machine available, so I took a swig of some stagnant bottled water. Time to hurry up and wait.

Eventually, the five-member band loaded their equipment in the van. But instead of taking off, they milled around, talking and smoking ganja, no sense of urgency at all.

Another half an hour passed. Finally, they climbed into the van. When it pulled out on to the street, I slowly followed behind them, keeping my distance.

Dark buildings, broken windows covered by bars. A few blocks away from the tourist hub, we were now in a shantytown. I couldn't help but fantasize that I was minutes away from seeing Annie again. That in only a few short hours, I'd be able to hold her and tell her that her nightmare was finally over.

After a few miles along the road, the van stopped in front of a one-story plantation-style house. It wasn't one of the brothels we'd investigated—I wasn't even sure if it was a brothel at all. No sign, no man out front, just a door with some metal bars on it and some lights in the windows. If it was a brothel, this one definitely wasn't one of the legal ones we'd been scoping out in the center of town.

Could Annie be in there?

The men got out. Four of them took off in a different parked old model sedan. Then the door to the house opened and the dancer walked inside and greeted another man.

I took out the binoculars I had stowed in the

glove compartment and his face came into focus. It was that pimp. The one I'd given my watch to, I was sure of it.

Fuck. Annie had to be in there. But was it a brothel? A drug den? Maybe it was a holding place where they drugged up the women before they moved them elsewhere. And how many men? I could see two—the pimp and dancer. But as far as I could tell, only the pimp was armed, with the same AK-47 he had in Aruba slung around his shoulders.

I drove my car around the building. In a window to the back, I could see a girl stare out the window. She had dark hair, but even with my binoculars that was all I could make out because she had left the window so quickly. Was she Annie? My gut told me she was, but there was only one way to find out.

I needed my men and my night-ops equipment. I drove back to the hotel, careful to mark the path in my mind.

I couldn't wait another day, another chance for them to move her. We had to move in tonight.

One desperate plea. This wasn't a Hollywood blockbuster or a New York Times best-selling thriller. I knew this time there was no room for excuses, no margin for errors. I had one chance to put the cape on and be her hero.

13. Patrick

I FLIPPED THE LIGHT ON in the hotel room. Kyle was passed out in the bed next to some blonde girl and Vic was crashed on the sofa in the small living area. I knew the drill—if one of us was going to get lucky, he'd head up to the room first. We'd hobble in later when the coast was clear and crash on the floor, giving the loving couple the bed. Of course, Vic never did that to us. He was a serial monogamist. We'd always tease him, but I was starting to think Kyle and I were the ones who were fucked up and Vic had the right idea. I wouldn't be in this mess now if I hadn't given in to my needs, but then again I would've never found Annie.

I nudged Kyle. "Hey. Sorry to interrupt. But we need to go."

Kyle understood. He rolled over to the girl. "Hey,

sweetheart. Sorry, but I need to help my buddy out."

The girl nodded, almost looked hurt. She reached for her clothes and got out of bed. I couldn't help but stare at her naked body. Great ass, perky tits, nice tan skin. She slipped her panties on, then her jeans, and pulled a pink tank top over her head. She either hadn't been wearing a bra or didn't bother to look for it. Kyle gave her a kiss on the cheek. "I'll call you. We'll be in town for a little while longer."

Kyle actually might call. He straddled the line of commitment-phobe and romantic. His usual M.O. was to start a fling with a girl, swear that she was the one, and then vanish when it got intense, which it always did. Everything we did was intense. Sometimes I wondered what it would be like to have a mellow job, a relaxed life.

I gave the girl an awkward wave. But because I was paranoid about Annie, I wanted to make sure she was going to be safe. "Where are you staying?"

"Oh, a hotel down the road. I'm fine to walk."

Fuck that. "We'll take you."

She looked at Kyle. "No, I'm okay. Really. It's just a few blocks."

Kyle got dressed. "No, Pat's right. Sorry, I should have offered myself. We'll drive you."

She shrugged her shoulders. "Okay."

She slipped into the bathroom. I signaled to the

guys to get their guns and night-op gear.

"It's on."

Vic slipped on his gun. "You found her?"

"Not sure. Her pimp is there." I explained about dancer and my watch.

"Good enough for me." Kyle loaded his pistol and gathered the bag full of our gear. "Hooyah!"

Kyle's girl walked out of the bathroom, her mascara smudged. But at that moment, I didn't see this nameless girl, I saw Annie. Annie's eyes. In one careless, drunken night, Annie's world had changed forever. Spring break, five years ago, a night like this. The girl who stood before me, she didn't know that Kyle was a good guy. That the three of us weren't going to gang rape her. But this girl took a chance, a chance on him, a chance with us. In a foreign country, with different laws. These girls had false senses of security, that they were invincible. But all it took was one wrong drink, one wrong man, and they could end up dead, or in a living hell. Just like Annie.

We headed out of the hotel and piled into the small rental car. We dropped the girl off at her hotel room, Kyle walking her in to make sure she was safe.

He climbed back into the car. "So what's the plan?"

"We're going to go back and case the place. I'm not even sure Annie is there."

This amateur rescue attempt was so different

than the missions we usually went on as a Team. We had to clear the house, like we'd done many times in Afghanistan. These traffickers probably only cared about drugs and money; they weren't going to risk their lives over one hooker. To them, Annie was property. Expendable.

We parked a block away from the building, put on our gear, and snuck up outside the door. The absence of sound and light made me believe everyone inside was asleep. I wanted this to be clean.

"I think she's in that room. Second window to the left."

"Let's check it out."

I was a non-practicing Catholic. Even so, every time I went on a mission, I always said a silent prayer.

Amen. Let's roll.

A dog barked in the distance. Kyle and Vic stood watch alongside me as I used my night vision goggles to peer into the window.

A sink, a bed, some rumpled sheets, a mop of dark hair. I focused the scope. Could I see her face? Her tattoo? The necklace?

She rolled to her side and her profile came into view. Annie was mere steps away from me, only metal bars and a bunch of lowlifes stood in between her and her freedom. My muscles trembled.

No time to celebrate—she wasn't free yet.

I signaled to my men. With those fucking bars

on her window, we couldn't just grab her. We had to go through the back door.

The execution of my duties will be swift and violent when required yet guided by the very principles that I serve to defend.

I had no intention to kill her captors. My only goal was to save Annie.

Gun and scope out, I touched the door. No lock. I pushed it in, and motioned for Vic and Kyle to follow. They were right behind me.

As they scanned for men, I crept down the hall to Annie's door.

She was sound asleep, under the covers. Or in a drugged stupor. If I woke her, would she scream?

Fuck it. I was about to scoop her limp body in my arms, when something under the covers moved.

A little boy.

Wavy hair, dark skin. Annie was cuddling his tiny body.

What the fuck?

Her eyes opened, startled. She clutched him to her chest.

"Who's that?" I whispered.

"My son. Please, take us away."

Her son? She didn't mention anything about a kid.

My heart almost pounded out of my chest. Lashes open, hazel eyes glowing. Color returned to her face. Her hope almost brought me to my knees.

I didn't have a choice and even if I had, I

wouldn't leave her little boy behind. I scooped them up, praying the little boy wouldn't wake. Who was his father? If he was the pimp or the dancer, how was I going to take the boy out of here without bloodshed?

We made it to the living room, and I immediately spied the pimp cowering in the corner. The dancer ducked behind the sofa.

A light went on; about a dozen half-naked women were huddled in the kitchen.

The pimp reached for his gun.

Stupid motherfucker.

Clickclickclick.

Kyle discharged his weapon with a second of hesitation.

A loud thud reverberated on the floor, the pimp's body now splayed on the ground. Women shrieked. The little boy's hazel eyes, the same shade as Annie's, opened yet he remained silent. The smell of gun smoke mixed with rotten food wafted through the air.

I shifted the boy to my other arm and placed Annie down, her legs shook so bad she dropped to the floor.

Vic gathered the women, crying and screaming, and secured them in a back room. Then, I handed him the little boy and Vic took him out of the room. He didn't need to see this.

Kneeling to the ground, I checked the pimp's

pulse. Gone.

"Secure!" Kyle yelled.

I aimed my gun at the dancer. As long as he didn't do anything dangerous, I'd let him live. His eyes cast a cold glance at Annie. An unspoken command.

Annie clutched my ankle. "Don't kill him!"

I didn't have time to deal with her attachment to her captor. I shook her off of my leg. "We don't want to hurt you, man. Forget you ever saw us. You have no idea who you're dealing with."

The dancer laughed. His hand lowered toward his waist, I didn't have time to disarm him. Too many lives were at stake.

Poppoppop.

His body collapsed forward.

"No!" Annie screamed and tried to run over to him. But I intercepted her and held her back, while Kyle checked the dancer. He was a goner.

I signaled to Kyle. "Send it."

He threw a stun grenade—we didn't want to take any chance of another armed man emerging from one of the rooms. A blinding light and booming sound reverberated, leaving anyone left disorientated.

Done. Let's get the fuck out of here.

Vic went in front of me; the little boy cradled in his arms, Kyle had my back. I walked out of that house, carrying Annie. My heartbeat drummed in my chest. I did it.

She was finally free.

We dashed into the car, then hightailed it out of there.

My Nation expects me to be physically harder and mentally stronger than my enemies. If knocked down, I will get back up, every time. I will draw on every remaining ounce of strength to protect my teammates and to accomplish our mission.

Annie held her son in her lap and rocked back and forth, tears streaming down her face. Her eyes, which had seemed so disturbed on the night I had met her, were soft, almost filled with an inner glow.

Why hadn't she told me about her son? Did she think I wouldn't save her if I'd known? Had I just killed his father?

She held my hand and refused to let go. I didn't want to let go of her either. I wanted to make sure Annie's pain had ended and I vowed to protect her until she was safe. This climax, this reunion, we'd both come down from this high soon. The invisible sand hourglass would run out before we both realized it.

14. Annie

THE CAR RACED DOWN THE road, and I didn't even look at the brothel in the rear view mirror. Was it finally in my past? Could I put this hell behind me?

I rolled down the window and breathed in the air.

Freedom.

The wave of emotions I expected to feel hadn't hit me yet. I wouldn't feel safe until I was back on American soil.

My baby cuddled up next to me; his warm skin trembled. I was all he had left—his father was dead. Killed by the man who I'd begged to rescue me. But I wouldn't shed a tear for my son's father, after the hell he put me through.

I stroked my son's hair, kissed his forehead. This wasn't about me, none of it. If it had only been me,

I'd have injected an air bubble in my vein years ago. In Gabriel's three short years, I'd been the best mom I could be to him, despite being a drug addict. I'd tried to quit, so many times, but his father had forced me to shoot up. Keeping me high was a way to control me, prevent me from escaping. And with possession of my son, I'd do anything he asked.

Gabriel would forever be a reminder of this life. But I loved him! Would anyone ever understand that? Would my family be able to accept him? How could I love the child of a monster? My captor? My kidnapper? A rapist?

Easy. Gabriel was innocent. My angel. He should not be held responsible for the sins of his father. Every cuddle, every "Mama," every kiss, every hug, made my heart flutter.

I whispered to Patrick. "I'm sorry I didn't tell you about my son."

He put his arm around me, his eyes remained fixed on the road ahead. "It's fine. I'll take care of you both as long as you need me to."

No anger, no hint of resentment, just calming words. Didn't he just kill someone? The father of my child? His steady demeanor chilled me. Who was this man sitting beside me? I had to remind myself he was a trained killer. This was his job.

My baby boy looked up at me, his big eyes brighter than usual. "Mama, where are we going?"

"Home, baby. We're going home."

15. Patrick

AFTER A PIT STOP AT our hotel to gather our stuff and check out, we drove Annie and her son straight to the yacht. I couldn't wait to get the fuck out of Curaçao. Kyle started up the boat to anchor it a few miles off the dock. We'd drop them off at the embassy in the morning, and then head back to Aruba in the afternoon, when the waters were calm.

I hadn't said much on the car ride. I'd just killed a man, possibly the little boy's father. No regret, but I needed a moment of silence.

Once we boarded the ship, I took Annie and her son to the living area. "Annie, these are my friends, Kyle and Vic. Vic's a medic; he's going to help start your detox. I bought you clothes and supplies."

She blinked rapidly, scanning the tiny room. She wore a tattered shirt, which skimmed her thighs, and black panties. She was skinny, almost deathly so. Her little boy was clad in an oversized tee shirt and gym shorts. I still hadn't heard him speak, and I prayed he wouldn't be forever traumatized by the violence of the rescue. Annie swayed with the movement of the boat, a little disoriented, probably in shock, and confused. Her flat black hair hung around her face and she hugged her arms tight to her chest. When she spoke, her voice was a whisper and cracked with emotion. "I didn't think I'd ever see you again. I can't ever thank you enough. I never, ever thought..."

She bit her lip in an attempt to stop the tears that shone in her eyes. She looked vulnerable and doll-like in the soft light of the room. I pulled her to me and held her close, her small frame tucked into my large one. She felt fragile in my huge arms, breakable. I took a steadying breath to stem the rising urge to keep her there, a feeling which pissed me off as much as it confused me.

"You're welcome. You don't have to thank me."

She didn't respond for a few moments, instead she tucked herself more closely into my embrace. I loathed to let her go, enjoying the feel of her soft body against mine when she took a step back.

I let out the breath I didn't know I was holding. I didn't know what the fuck I'd expected her reaction to be. I guess I thought she'd be running around ecstatic, kissing and hugging me, but her dull calm threw me. I had to remind myself she was an addict, and the reality of her freedom hadn't sunk in for her yet.

The little boy remained quiet.

Annie watched me eye him. "His name is Gabriel. He's three and a half."

I didn't have a fucking clue what to say to him. "Hey, buddy. I'm Pat."

He wrapped his body around Annie's leg. I handed her the duffel bag I'd prepared for her. She murmured thank you and walked slowly into the bathroom, her little boy trailing her, and shut the door.

I pulled out a bottle of whiskey from my sea bag, throwing back a quick shot. What the fuck had I gotten us into?

If this had been a movie, we would've whisked her to the embassy, her parents waiting to greet her. I'd have a hero's welcome. We'd profess our love to each other and go on to live happily ever after.

But this wasn't a movie. This rescue was off the books. The embassy in Curaçao was closed because it was the middle of the night and on the weekend. I didn't even know her. And our victim was a heroin-addicted prostitute with a child.

Vic took some meds out of his bag. "So, it's going to be a rough detox, especially for the next seventy-two hours. And now we have her son to take care of. We'll keep her comfortable. Did you know about the kid? Who was the dad?"

"Of course I didn't know. Not a fucking clue who the father is." I heard water run. What was going through her head now? Her family, her friends, me?

Kyle laughed. "Dude, you pulled this off. Do you get how crazy this shit is? I mean, she's been missing for five years, presumed dead. I never doubted you. Are you going to claim the reward?"

Three hundred thousand dollars. I made around sixty thousand a year. A pittance considering the fact I risked my life every day. Killed for my country. Could die for my country. I could use the money. Buy my mom a nicer house. Maybe save up some for my retirement, when I'd probably be so physically and mentally fucked up that I wouldn't be able to hold down a job. But I didn't want a cent. That's not why I did what I did. Why any of us did.

"Nope. Not going to touch it. I hope to hell Annie will keep our involvement out of the press. But I'm prepared to face the consequences if our command finds out."

Take responsibility for your actions and the actions of your teammates.

We'd already covered this ground—I wouldn't have brought them into this if I was going to shout about it from the rooftops—but it was done now and they needed to know I was committed to that.

"Well, I doubt they'd discipline us for saving an American girl who was sex trafficked and her son born into captivity. The media would have a field day with that. 'Navy SEALs punished for saving America's Sweetheart and innocent boy.' I say you collect the reward. I'll take my share. I need a new truck."

"What-the-fuck-ever, man. You're loaded with all your NFL money. Anyway, not going to happen."

I do not advertise the nature of my work nor seek recognition for my actions.

Annie emerged from the bathroom, clutching Gabriel. She'd changed into the sweat suit I'd bought her.

Her son finally spoke. "Mommy sad." He wrapped his arms around her.

"I'm going to get him to sleep."

"Hey, wait." I pulled that teddy bear I'd taken from the rubble out of my sea bag, and handed it to Gabriel. "Is this yours?"

Gabriel smiled. "Bear!" He squeezed the bear.

Annie's mouth dropped. "Thank you. He'd been asking about it but I thought it was gone forever."

Glad I could give the kid some kind of comfort.

I showed them the bedroom. Kyle and Vic went to the top deck to get some fresh air and I waited in the living room for Annie.

Around an hour later, she emerged from the bedroom. She sat at the table and ate some chips I had out.

I sat there in silence, staring. What the fuck do we do now?

After a sip of water, she burst into tears.

I went over and sat next to her. "Hey, it's okay."

"No, it's not okay. I don't know what to do, who I am. I mean, I'm a drug addict. I was a prostitute. My family won't want me back. Look at me! To get a clean vein, I've been shooting up in my feet! And what if they don't accept Gabriel?"

Fuck. I had mentally prepared myself for her anxiety and detox, but I didn't want to give her any false hope. Being rescued was the easy part; she would need to rebuild her life. She needed to see herself as I saw her—a beautiful survivor.

I took a deep breath, knowing I needed her to hear me. "You are strong, a survivor. After the hell you've been through, you can do anything. I'm sure of it. And your parents love you. How could they not love your child? They've been looking for you non-stop. I'm sure they'll help you every step of the way. I'm going to take you to the embassy tomorrow when we dock. You will be safe there."

Her hands clenched. "You're leaving me at the embassy? Where do you think my clients come from? I've serviced heads of state, secret service, diplomats. Renzo's sex ring runs the island. And they could try to say Gabriel is a Dutch National. We could spend years fighting with the government. You might as well throw me off this boat."

"He's an American citizen also. It's an American embassy, you'll be fine. I'll walk you in. They will contact your family."

Her chin quivered, her eyes fluttered. She looked embarrassed, vulnerable. "You can't take me with you?"

"No, I can't Annie. I would, but we flew here commercially. You don't have a passport—we can't get you aboard a flight. We're on Navy leave—all of us."

I decided not to mention there were Navy carriers docking in port weekly and Kyle, Vic, and I could always hitch a ride. But she and Gabriel couldn't. Well, that wasn't exactly true—there was one way I could bring her with me, keep her safe—if I married her. But that was never going to happen. I never wanted to get married, and I didn't even know this girl, despite my desire to take care of her, and protect her for the rest of her life. And forget marriage, after the unspeakable hell she'd been through, I doubted she would ever want to date any man, let alone one of her former clients. Not to mention, she had a son. After being the son of a single mom, I wouldn't even consider messing around with one unless I was one hundred percent certain the relationship was going to work. I'd been that kid, and there was no way I was going to let some little boy get attached to me, and then bail.

"I won't go. Please, don't send me back like this. Maybe we can sail back? In this yacht? You're a SEAL? Please!"

"Sail back? It would take a couple of weeks. This

isn't even our boat—we borrowed it from a former Team guy. We don't have supplies, or anything. And you could get sick, you'll be detoxing."

Her head shook, she bit her lip. "But you could do it right? You said Vic's a medic, right? I'll be fine."

I shook my head. "You have to go to the embassy."

Rising from the chair, her eyes focused on me, intent, desperate. I knew that look. It was the look that I had, that my men had when they were determined to get their way. Determined not to quit. No matter what the cost.

She walked over to my chair and knelt beside me. Her hand inched up my leg, rubbing my cock over my jeans. "I'll do anything. Please. Help me."

I pushed her hand off me. Fuck, she still saw me as nothing more than another john who would use her for sex. I wasn't that guy. She was nameless to me before, but now I cared about what happened to her. Especially since she was a mother. I pulled her into my arms. "Annie, you don't ever, ever have to touch me like that again. I'm not that guy. I can't apologize enough to you. But I came back. I found you. That's what matters." I paused. I really needed to send her to the embassy as soon as possible, but the tears stuck in her lashes made me unable to tell her no. "I'll talk to Dave. He owns the ship. I can't promise you anything but he's a former SEAL and a local. He might be able to come up with something. But I promise you, I'll get you home safely."

"Can we stay here, on this boat, until I detox? I need to get my mind clear before I go back. I don't want my family to see me like this. And I can't watch Gabriel if I'm going out of my mind. I need help."

I should've checked with Vic and Kyle first, but I knew they would want the best for her kid. "Sure, of course. We'll stay with you until you detox."

She took my hand. "I'm scared. I've wanted to get clean, but Renzo forced me to get high. I need it."

"You survived five years of unspeakable hell. You can do this. You are stronger than you know. We're going to help you. I promise I won't leave your side."

I got Vic and he took her into the bathroom, tested her for STDs, HIV, and pregnancy. The tests gave instant results, and we were all grateful and, well, shocked when she tested negative for everything. Prostitution was legal and officially regulated in the Dutch Caribbean, so Annie claimed she'd been tested and used condoms. Vic rationed out her drug cocktail: immodium, suboxone, Xanax, vitamins, potassium. He gave her the first dose and she downed the pills with a glass of water.

I held her hand. "I think you should sleep if you can."

She nodded her head and leaned into me. I picked her up off the chair and carried her to the bedroom with the queen bed, her boy already fast asleep. I'd planned to crash on the floor next to her. I pulled a blanket from the closet and set it down on the floor for me.

"Patrick, can you hold me? Just until I fall asleep."

I couldn't say no. It was her first night free in five years. I couldn't even begin to imagine how scared she might be, even now when she was safer than she'd been in a long time. "Sure." I wrapped my arms around her and she cuddled up into my chest. Her body rattled a bit, clammy and limp. After a bit, she drifted off to sleep. I felt like if I moved at all, I'd break her. She was fragile, small, and weak. I was spooning her, her curves rubbing against me. Once she rolled over, I made my escape and lay down on the floor.

This was going to be a long night.

I couldn't remember the last time I'd spent the night in the same room with a woman instead of darting away in the middle of the night. I fought sleep as long as I could, looking over at the slight girl and her son asleep on the bed, praying they would be okay.

16. Patrick

THE BED RATTLED AND THE vibrations from the floor awoke me from sleep. My first thought was it was an angry wave, until I realized it was Annie who was shaking. Her little boy popped up in bed, his hair disheveled, and let out a whimper. She ran to the bathroom and slammed the door.

I didn't know what the fuck to do. I sat on the bed next to Gabriel.

"Hey buddy, you want to check out the boat?"

I had nothing to offer him—totally ill-equipped to entertain a toddler. No toy trains or cars. No crayons or stickers. I didn't want to touch him, scare him. I hadn't a clue what kind of life he'd grown accustomed to, who took care of him while Annie worked. Fuck—I still didn't know who his dad was, and for that matter, if I'd killed him.

I could hear Annie gagging and retching.

Gabriel looked around the room, his eyes fixed on the tiny porthole.

"Boat?" he said.

"Yes—we're on a boat. Do you want to see it?"

He nodded and put his arms around my neck. His affection startled me, so trusting, so warm. I carried him to the deck where Kyle was manning the ship.

"Hey, little man." Kyle came from a big family with a bunch of nieces and nephews. "You want to help me steer?"

A smile broke out on Gabriel's face. Kyle offered his hand to Gabriel, and the little boy happily took it, and stepped up to the control panels.

Kyle turned to me, "I got this. Anyway, we need to talk about what we're going to do with them."

Vic interjected. "She's right, you know. We can't drop her off at the embassy, with her son. He's a Dutch National. They could prevent him from leaving the country."

"I know. What are our options?"

Kyle spoke, his hands helping Gabriel steer the wheel. "We can sail her back to San Diego."

"No way. We don't have the supplies, it will take at least two weeks, and I've never sailed through the Panama Canal. She's detoxing. This isn't even our boat."

Vic stretched out on the deck. "We don't have a

choice, Walsh. Unless you marry her and take them on a Navy cruiser. The consulate might try to locate Gabriel's family, might investigate our mission at the brothel. I already radioed Dave. I didn't give him the details about Annie, but I asked him if there was any way we could take the boat to San Diego. He said yes—as long as we took him."

Great, just fucking great. Not exactly the way I wanted to spend the few weeks of leave I get a year. But they were right. I didn't have a choice. I'd see this mission through to the end. And I trusted Dave, we'd used his weapons for the rescue anyway. "Fine. Let's go tell Annie. Kyle, radio Dave and confirm everything. Make sure he gets enough supplies for us, Annie, and the boy. Toys and stuff, too."

Kyle grabbed the radio. "Roger that. Go take care of Annie."

Vic headed back to the room with me, carrying his medical bag. "How's she doing?"

"She woke up and puked."

We entered the room; Annie was sitting on the bed, her hair wet, her skin bluish.

Vic gave her more meds, and she calmed down for a bit. He then went to the kitchen to make us all breakfast.

I led Annie into the living area. I warmed some chicken broth in a mug and handed her a banana, which was about the extent of my cooking skills. "You need to eat. Here."

She took a sip of the broth and relaxed into the

chair. "I thought I was dreaming. I can't believe I'm really free. When we moved islands, I thought my one chance was gone forever. How did you find me?"

I studied the girl sitting in front of me. She already looked different to me than she had when I'd last seen her in the brothel. She seemed lighter, like a weight had been lifted from her soul. But her skin was pale and her hair was lifeless. She still had a long way to go before she fully returned to the land of the living. "I went back to the brothel in Aruba—it was burnt to the ground. We searched the island for you and Kyle got a tip that you girls were moved to Curaçao, so we came here. You'd told me the last thing you remembered at the resort was being in the elevator with that dancer. He was playing at a bar and I followed him. I thought I saw you in the window, so I took a chance and here we are."

Sweat dripped from her forehead. "That's amazing. You're amazing. How can I ever thank you? My dad, he has money..."

I raised my hand up. "Stop. I'm not interested in money. Your father has offered a reward, a huge one at that, but I don't want it. In fact, the only way you can thank me is never mentioning our involvement in your rescue."

She winced. "Oh, okay. I get it. You don't want to be associated with me. I understand."

"That's not it. We all need to be anonymous to do our jobs in the Teams. And this was off-record. We didn't get permission from our command. We could get disciplined and ruin our careers."

Her eyes closed and her jaw shook. "So I have to lie about how I was rescued?"

"I'm not asking you to lie. But you need to leave our names out of it. Our names and pictures can't be plastered over the media or we'll get kicked out of the Teams. We can't exactly go undercover if the world knows our identities."

She took a small bite of the banana. "I get it. I'm sorry I got you involved in this."

I touched her shoulder. "Hey. Don't say that. I'm not sorry. I'm not sorry about any of it. How I met you, that you told me your name, or how I found you. I'm only sorry I didn't torture the motherfuckers who took you." I paused ... I had to ask about Gabriel. "Your son—his dad?"

"Renzo, the dancer." Her eyes seemed distant and dare I say, sad. "You didn't have to kill him."

"Are you fucking serious? I actually would've let him go, but he reached for his weapon. Cocky motherfucker was laughing. My only goal was to save you and your son. Especially now, knowing he was the boy's father, he could've tried to kill us all since we were taking his son away. He kidnapped you. How can you even say that?"

I couldn't read her. Her mouth was turned downward in a frown yet she was nodding her head. "Renzo wasn't that bad compared to the others. He took care of me."

This poor fucking girl was identifying with her captor. I'd studied that shit. "Annie, he was a fucking pimp. He sold you."

"I know. But sometimes he was nice to me, like when I was pregnant. And he was good to Gabriel." Her eyes shifted. "Sorry, it's just hard for me."

Jesus, this girl needed some serious psychotherapy. I knew she'd be messed up, but she seemed to care more about Renzo's well-being than her own. Or her son's.

"We're going to sail you to San Diego. It will take a couple of weeks."

She beamed at me. "Oh, Patrick. Thank you. You truly are a hero."

I hated being called a hero. This was my job. Any Team guy would've done the same. "You're welcome. I need you to focus on getting better. Somehow I don't think this journey will help with the detox."

"I can do it. I'm not scared of anything. Now that I know we're going home."

She wouldn't be saying that tomorrow, when the withdrawal kicked in. But I would be here for her, every step of the way.

"Where's Gabriel?"

"On the deck with Kyle."

"Can I see him?"

"Of course. You don't have to ask me permission to do anything. You're safe here."

Pushing herself off the chair, she walked over to me and kissed me on the cheek. "I know I'm safe. You're here."

She climbed down the stairs to the deck and stood there in the breeze, breathing in the Caribbean air. Gabriel ran up to her and she scooped him in her arms, pointing at the ocean. He kissed his mama. I could see she loved him, that she didn't see him as the son of her captor, just as her adorable little boy.

I wanted to ask her a thousand questions, about her life before she was taken, about the horror she had endured, but I was in too deep already.

17. Patrick

WE MET DAVE ON THE dock, just after sunset, avoiding customs and immigration. We didn't want anyone questioning us. Dave loaded food, water, supplies, and toys for Gabriel. I instructed Annie to keep Gabriel in the bedroom until we headed back out to sea.

Dave took helm of the ship, and we set out on our journey to San Diego. Before I could open my mouth to debrief him, he gave me a wink. "You found her? That missing American? Annie?"

"Yes. In a brothel in Aruba. How the hell did you know?"

"I've been looking for her myself. Hoping to claim the reward. But I never got anywhere. You aren't the first treasure hunters to come searching for her pile of gold. A few years ago, some other former Team guys showed up here, sniffing around."

Other guys? "You mean the con man? The one who bilked her dad out of money?"

"No. Not that fraud. These other men. Team guys—not active like you. Older. Retired. They were here for a full month, rented one of my yachts. But they came up empty handed also."

So her parents had hired private security contractors to find her? That didn't make any sense. I found her and wasn't even looking. And even when I lost her, I'd found her again within a week. Something didn't add up.

"Dave, we didn't come here for the reward money. I found Annie myself. I hired her in a brothel when our ship docked. And we can't take the money or be in the papers because of the rescue. You'd actually help us out if you took credit."

Dave stared at me dead-on. "You're fucking with me."

"No, I'm dead serious. Collect the reward. I don't want to get kicked out of the Teams. It's my life—all I have. My career is just beginning. Take it—it's yours."

He shook my hand. "You have my word, kid. I'll make sure you stay out of the papers, and I'll reimburse you for this entire trip. If you ever need anything, money or anything, please, what's mine is yours."

"I appreciate that, man." I heard a thump down

below. "I need to check on Annie."

I walked down to her room. "Pat! Pat!" Annie was pacing around the cabin.

Fuck. She was withdrawing, hard. Her skin was almost yellowish and she was pulling out her hair. I opened the door. "Kyle, can you show Gabriel his new toys?"

"Sure thing." Kyle rummaged through the bags Dave brought. He held up a toy ship. "Little man, you want to play with this boat?"

Gabriel trotted over to Vic, who took him to the other room. From now on, I had to do a better job of shielding Gabriel from his mother's detox.

I sat on Annie's bed. "What? What's wrong?"

Her hands trembled, her teeth clattered. "I need a fucking fix. Can you get me some smack? Maybe we can sail back and find a dealer. Just a little? I can't do this. I can detox at home! My dad will send me to one of those Hollywood country club kinds of rehabs."

Calm, Pat. Stay calm. "No way am I going to score you dope. And if you haven't noticed, we're in the middle of the ocean. You can do this, Annie. You need to do this for Gabriel."

Vic opened the door to our room and tried to hand her more meds, but she pushed them out of his hand and they scattered on the floor.

Vic bent over to grab them but I stopped him. "Annie, pick them up," I said calmly but firmly.

"You can't fucking tell me what to do," she

hissed. Her pupils were dilated and she had beads of sweat on her forehead.

Vic was about to speak, but I signaled to him that I would handle it.

I still didn't raise my voice. "I said pick them up, Annie."

She cackled. "I don't have to listen to you. You don't fucking own me. You're no hero—so fucking pathetic you have to pay for a blowjob from a whore. You're no better than my pimp. At least he kept me high. At least he could stomach fucking me. I know you want me. What the fuck is your problem? Can't get it up?"

My muscles quivered. I wasn't going to engage with her. She was detoxing. I had to remind myself this was normal.

"I'm not going to ask you again. Pick them up or I'll flush them down the toilet. You need them. They will make you feel better."

She spat in my face then crawled on the floor and got the pills. This wasn't Annie, this was Star. Like a fucking Jekyll and Hyde.

The ability to control my emotions and my actions, regardless of circumstance, sets me apart from other men.

Vic handed her water and she downed the pills. Then she went into the bathroom, slammed the door, and started the shower.

Vic spoke in a quiet voice. "This is normal, man. My cousin went through this. He fucking jumped off a balcony trying to score."

I gave a heavy nod. Her son had been born into hell. He needed his mom to be strong. I accepted this project with no reservations.

18. Annie

MY BODY FLUNG OUT OF the bed like I was possessed. My flesh burned; I clawed at my skin, biting my arms, trying to gnaw away the agony.

Pat shot up from his makeshift bed on the floor.

"I can't fucking do this, Pat." My nails raked at the skin on my forearms. I rubbed a palm on my thigh. "I can't. I can't. It's too hard. You can take me back, I don't fucking care. I need it. It hurts."

I crumpled to my knees, grating against the rough wood floor, breathing through my breathless sobs. Pat crouched beside me and laid a hand against my back, which was clammy with sweat. I shrieked at his touch and cringed backwards.

"Don't fucking touch me!" The sound of my scream echoed off the walls of the room. "Don't touch me. I don't want anyone to touch me."

Pat didn't give up that easily.

I shivered. He wrapped me in a blanket and held me. I resisted at first, and then fell into his arms, searching for relief. Strong, warm, secure. Could he just hold me forever? This patient, kind man. The way he looked at me, the way he took care of my son and me. Why was he helping me, what would I owe him? How could he not want something in return?

Dizzy and lightheaded, I almost left my body. His lips pressed on my forehead and he rocked me until I fell asleep.

19. Patrick

FOR SEVENTY-TWO HOURS, SHE went through a merciless detox. The paranoia had set in; it was brutal to watch her suffering, her body quivering. She had her rough moments, where she didn't want to get out of bed—screaming, crying, and pleading for her next fix. She flipped from being a sweet, yet reserved girl, to a paranoid drug fiend.

Through it all, I tried to be there for her, give her anything she needed, talk her down from the highs, up from the lows. Her behavior didn't upset or concern me. I knew she would get through this. She'd survived worse.

The heroin had finally left her body, like a ghost of her nightmare.

Kyle, Vic, Dave, and I all did our best to keep Gabriel occupied and away from Annie. During her lucid phases, she explained Gabriel's grandmother and aunts watched him while she worked. So he was used to being away from her. They would have to rebuild their entire relationship once Annie was healthy.

Kyle, Vic, and I were crammed in the living area, watching television while Gabriel played with a cheap train set Dave had bought him. It didn't even bother my brothers that they had given up their entire vacation leave to help this girl. I was thankful for them, for my training, and for my ability to have the tactical skills to save Annie.

"Vroom, vroom." Gabriel pushed his little train around the tracks. "Pat, do it!"

I knelt on the floor. I knew the deal—Gabriel wanted me to race his train around the track with another train, but let him win.

The little boy let out a laugh. I was happy to see him smile, not sure of what kind of life he'd known back in the Caribbean. I had to admit, at first, I saw him as a burden. A living reminder of Annie's ordeal. But now I saw him as this cute little boy, the light of Annie's life.

I didn't want to get attached to him or him to get attached to me. I couldn't understand the men who dated my mom, played trains with me when I was his age, made me look up to them, and then abandoned us. I never knew where they went, and used to ask my mom when they would be coming back.

Annie awoke and walked into the living area. She played with Gabriel for a bit, then got him ready for bed, and put him to sleep in her room. Vic handed her water and her meds, and she pushed back her crazy hair and gave me that crooked smile I had first noticed in the lineup that day.

"How are you feeling?" She already look better; her skin brighter, her eyes wider.

She nodded her head. "Good. Better. Thanks for taking care of me."

"Don't worry about it." Vic and Kyle headed up to the deck. I wanted to go and hang out with them. "We're going to be home in two days. Are you excited?"

"No. Scared. Anxious. I don't know how my parents will react to Gabriel."

"They'll love him. He's a great boy."

"You don't understand. My parents are good people, but they aren't that warm. My dad wants everything to be perfect, you know? A bastard child whose dad was a sex trafficker doesn't really fit into that picture."

I didn't know what to say to reassure her. I was sure she was wrong, though. Who wouldn't love that boy? It wasn't his fault his father was a jackass. My father was a complete loser, also. And my mom would love any child I brought home, no matter what the circumstances were.

Annie's eyes narrowed at me. "Why did you do

this, Pat?"

"Do what?"

"Help me detox. I mean, Vic is giving me meds, but why do you hold me at night, rock me to sleep?"

I didn't even know why myself. "You've been through enough. Gabriel needs his mom to be strong. You're all he has—I killed his dad, who, granted, was a piece of shit. It's the right thing to do."

"So that's it? You're going to take me to my parents' house, and I'll never see you again?" Her voice trailed off.

"Yup. That's the plan. I leave for training a week after you get back." Truth was, I was stationed in Coronado, so when I came off deployment, I could technically see her again. Her family lived nearby in Encinitas. But that wouldn't be a good idea. I trained sometimes eighteen hours a day and spent my time off at SEAL watering holes, like Danny's Palm Bar & Grill. She wouldn't find me hanging out at the country club with her friends that was for damn sure.

"What's your deal? Why don't you have a girlfriend or a wife? You're a SEAL. All my sorority sisters would always go SEAL hunting in Coronado and drop their panties in seconds if there were any sightings. You're gorgeous, sexy, selfless...any girl would be lucky to have you."

Tell that to my ex. "Not really. I had a girl and she cheated on me. I'm a great SEAL, but I'm a lousy boyfriend. I'm never around, I can't provide for anyone emotionally. I'm just not interested in a relationship. Not until I retire. I can't be responsible for anyone else when I'm thousands of miles away. And my job is dangerous. I won't get married while I'm in because if anything happened to me, I wouldn't want to leave a kid without a dad, like mine did to me."

She winced. Fuck, how could I've said that?

After an uncomfortable pause, she started again with her questions. "He was a SEAL, too?"

"No. He was a deadbeat who couldn't take any responsibility for his actions."

She put her hand on my shoulder, trying to comfort me. But I pushed it off. "I need to get some fresh air. I'll be on the deck if you need anything."

She shrugged her shoulders. "Okay. Good night." She went back into her room, laid in the bed and pulled the covers over her head.

I needed a break from her, from this intensity. I wanted everything to be normal, my normal, before I'd ever set foot in that brothel.

Safe on the deck with no child or woman, Vic handed me a beer. "You good?"

"Yup." I took a sip and sat down. I didn't even know how to process all the emotions I was going through. It had been so long since I'd had to think about a woman's fucking feelings.

Kyle grabbed his own beer and sat next to me. "So, she seems better. Have you tapped that yet?"

Vic just shook his head. "What this fucker means is you aren't getting too close, are you?"

"Fuck that, Vic. I just want to know if he's gotten laid. They've been alone plenty while we've been babysitting and Annie's clearly in love with him. We're trapped out in the middle of the ocean, with only one girl and three of us, four if you count Dave. If I'm not getting any, at least he should be. I mean, you're sleeping in the same room with her every night. Those walls are thin, but damned if I don't hear any headboards banging."

"You're both fucking idiots. She just detoxed off heroin. She's a recovering sex slave. What kind of sick fuck would sleep with her right now knowing what she's been through? I'm not in love and I'm not going to fuck her. Not now, not ever. Plus, I'd never do that to her little boy. I fucking killed his father. I'm not going to marry his mother. This isn't Shakespeare. That boy's going to be fucked up enough, he doesn't need me popping in and out of his life. She's not in love with me; she's just attached to me because I saved her. She'll forget all about me once she's acclimated back to her life. She's got someone waiting anyway. Probably. He says he is."

Kyle laughed. "That chump girly-man surfer? Please. He can't compete with you. You're a motherfucking SEAL, asshole."

Vic motioned his hand toward me as if he was my fucking therapist. "So, you're trying to tell me you have no feelings for her? At all?"

"That's what I'm saying. I don't know her, really. I mean, half the time she's out of her mind crazy, detoxing. The other half she's all moody and withdrawn. She's hot, for sure, but I don't have a clue who she is. I don't even think she knows who she is."

"So you haven't slept with her?" Kyle asked.

"Are you deaf? What the fuck did I just say? I mean, I fucking met her at a brothel and paid her to blow me. I seriously doubt she's interested in any man after what she's been through."

Vic put his arm around me. "You're a good man, Walsh. When you get back to San Diego after our next training, you guys can meet up again and see if you have any common ground."

"Not going to happen. I don't want to remind her of this. I was one of her clients. She and Gabriel need someone stable. And that sure as hell isn't me."

"But you deserve to be happy. Not all girls are going to cheat on you like Marissa did."

"Whatever, man. Your wife cheated on you, too. I know hardly anyone in the Teams with a good marriage. The only guys who make it work are married to their high school sweethearts. Mine cheated on me, so game over. And it's not just about that.

Annie is so messed up. She's going to need a man who can be with her, take care of her, and protect her. I can never be that man."

Kyle pounded his beer and looked down toward the guest quarters. "That's the thing. You rescued her. You've been taking care of her. You're already that man, whether you like it or not."

Shit. I came up here to relax. Now I wanted to jump overboard. Fucking idiots.

The three of us had spent so many hours together in silence, watching targets, waiting for action. They knew me better than I knew myself. I couldn't deny the connection I had with Annie, the sense we were meant to find each other. I wasn't talking about some crappy, romantic movie instalove, just this intense feeling we were destined to be in each other's lives. I saved her and her son. That was enough for me.

The gentle waves rocked beneath me. I laid down under the stars and drifted to sleep.

20. Annie

TONIGHT WAS OUR LAST NIGHT together. Tomorrow, he would drive me to my parents' house, and then vanish from my life. Move on to his next mission. Would I ever see him again?

For our last night, we ported in Ensenada, Mexico, though Pat wouldn't let me get off the yacht and risk being seen. Kyle, Dave, and Vic had gone into town and taken Gabriel. I was grateful they all loved my little boy and were taking him somewhere fun before the inevitable media circus would make us prisoners in my own home. They'd be back later, but for the first time since this ordeal had begun, Pat and I were completely alone.

We sat at the tiny table in the corner of the room. Pat plugged in his phone so we had some music—classic rock not classical. I didn't think he was trying to set a seduction scene, but it felt like a romantic date. He was so handsome and rugged. I saw him with fresh eyes—not the man who'd hired me to blow him, not the SEAL who rescued me, just this strong, sensitive, masculine man. A man who would kill to protect me—and he already had.

Pat had snuck out into town before the others left and brought in food from a local restaurant. He'd been raving this entire trip about how he couldn't wait for me to try the lobster. Pretty sweet of him. Nearby Puerto Nuevo was a fishing village, which was famous for its lobster, so we had lobster, fresh homemade tortillas, and all the fixings. My taste buds were alive. It was the best food I'd had in years: the plump flesh of the lobster, the buttery tortillas, and the creamy guacamole. I was craving a strawberry margarita, but Pat didn't think it was a good idea—he felt it was too soon for me to drink alcohol since I was recovering. But, all in all, it was a perfect meal. I guess it was kind of a celebration. A toast to getting my life back.

He poured me a glass of Mexican cola. "What's the first thing you're going to do when you get home?"

I lifted the glass and pressed my lips onto it. I felt his eyes watching me, watching my lips. "Oh, I don't know. Sounds weird, but I don't want to see my friends for a while. I'm sure they're all going to act weird around me, or ask me all sorts of crazy questions that I don't want to answer. Nicole used to joke that if we ever got rescued, it would be like winning the Super Bowl. You know, 'You've just won the Super Bowl. What are you going to do next? I'm going to Disneyland.' But that's not really my thing. I'd love to take Gabriel to Lake Tahoe, walk around the lake. Something outside. I've been locked up for so long; I'm desperate to just get out, walk, hike, and bike on the trails. Be free."

His mouth widened into a smile. "That's exactly what I like to do in my free time. Anything out in nature, hiking, camping, exploring. I grew up going to Lake Tahoe every summer."

"Oh? Really? Maybe we ran into each other? My parents have a vacation home in Incline Village."

Pat shook his head. "They have a place in Incline? Sure they do. I doubt you ever saw me on your private beach. My mom made sure that even though money was always tight, she would save up enough for us to spend a week in a crappy motel in Lake Tahoe every summer. You know, the kind across the street from Denny's with an above ground pool."

I started biting my nails. What an idiot I was, talking about my summer home. Pat clearly didn't grow up with money. I never had considered myself a snob before I'd been taken, but I was quite aware my parents were pretentious. They expected me to marry a man from a stable two-parent home, the son of doctors or lawyers. I shivered; how would they ever accept Gabriel?

Pat's eyes watched me. He was so in tune with my emotions. Was this from his training? I felt like he could read my mind.

He changed the subject. "I have a week in San Diego before we leave again. I'm just going to spend time with my dog, Trigger. He was one of our military dogs in Iraq. He's a German Shepherd. Retired. Great dog. One of the SEAL BUD/S instructors takes care of him when I'm gone. Here's a pic of him."

He took out his iPhone and showed me a pic of a huge dog.

"He's gorgeous. I want to meet him. Are you going home to visit your mom? Where are you from anyway?" I realized I didn't know anything about Pat, except, of course, he was a SEAL.

"Sacramento. I was going to, but I don't have any time. Have to get my life in order before we go. I've been gone for six months, then this one month leave, and we're heading out for another three months."

I pushed my food around my plate. "I'm sorry I took up all your vacation time."

"Don't be." He took my hand across the table, shivers radiated through my body. I knew rationally that I was having feelings for him because he saved me, nothing more. But I couldn't help the fact I'd dreamt of this beautiful man every night since I met him. I was sure he was destined to save me, destined to choose me. But the way he treated me during the boat ride, with kid gloves, also made me confident his only feelings toward me were those of protection, compassion, and pity.

"Pat, I'm scared of going home. I wish I could stay here on this yacht. With you."

"Why are you scared? Your parents are going to be thrilled to see you. I can't imagine their pain." He paused and released my hand. "And your boyfriend has given interviews about how he's still in love with you. I'm sure you two will run off and get married. Live happily ever after and have two point five kids with a minivan."

"Chris? Please. I mean he's a good guy. He's a surfer, used to get high all the time. I feel really bad about everything he's been through, people thinking he killed me and all. But I'm so different now. He's not the type of man I can see myself with. I want to be with someone strong, caring, and brave." I paused and took Pat all in. I wanted to know everything about this man. What he felt, what he thought, what made him tick? "You're incredible, you know that, right? Not many men would've returned to save me."

"You're a job to me, Annie. A mission. An American. I'm a SEAL, this is what I do. Any of the other guys on the Teams would do the same thing. It doesn't make me special."

He saw me as nothing more than a mission. And his mission was almost over. "Have you ever been in love?"

He looked away. "Yup. Once. She cheated. End of story."

No matter how hard I tried, he wouldn't open up to me. "Whatever. There's always more to the story. Maybe she cheated on you because you're so closed off. I mean, I've been living with you for two weeks and you know everything about me. But I don't know a thing about you. Except that you're a SEAL. You never fail to remind me of that."

"So, that's an excuse to cheat on me? While I'm out getting shot at by the Taliban?"

"No, of course not. Not all girls cheat. I never cheated on Chris. But if you never let your ex in, she probably felt lonely. Like I feel now."

"Fine, what do you want to know?"

He took a sip of his beer, his lips hovering over the glass. I imagined those lips on mine, what it would feel like to be desired instead of used. I had to push that thought out of my mind. "That's not how it works. This isn't an interrogation. I don't want to know anything. I want to understand you."

"I hate talking about myself, but if it's important to you, I'll try."

He remained silent.

"Why did you want to become a SEAL?"

"They're the best of the best. When I was a kid, one of my mom's boyfriends threw her up against a wall and broke her shoulder. I wanted to kill that motherfucker. I guess I never wanted to feel powerless again."

I choked back the tears, not willing to let him see me looking weak yet again. Would Gabriel have memories of his dad yelling at me? Forcing me to take drugs? Seeing me walk down the hallway with different men and disappearing for hours?

Pat was staring at me again with that look where he was trying to anticipate my thoughts. "I admire your strength. I don't know how many women could go through what you went through and still be able to smile."

A rush of desire overtook me. I wanted this man, couldn't stop fantasizing about him. I didn't want him to look at me as a victim—I wanted him to see me as a woman.

I glanced around the room, then fixated on him. It was our last night together; would I ever see him again? I had nothing to lose. "Pat, I have one favor to ask."

He didn't hesitate. "Anything. Shoot."

My mouth widened into a smile, and I moistened my lips. "Make love to me."

His eyes bugged out, and he shifted in his seat. "Annie, you're beautiful, and in any other situation, *any other situation*, I would love to make love to you. But we can't go there. I don't want to hurt you. And I'm incapable of offering you any more than a one-night stand and you deserve more. I deploy at least nine months out of the year. When I'm home, I'm so tired from training. Your first experience after this nightmare should be special."

My lips parted, I stood up and walked over to him. "I know what I want. I understand your job. For the past five years, I've been forced to have sex with strangers, do unthinkable things. Drugged out of my mind." I leaned into him and ran my fingers through his hair. "Don't let the last memory I have of being with a man, be of someone who paid for me. Someone I was unable to reject. I want you. I choose you. Make me feel good."

For a second, I thought he would take me up on my offer. His eyes looked at me with hunger; I could see him growing with desire. My hand inched up his thigh and I stroked him. I wanted to feel him inside of me; for him to make me scream his name and make me come. I wanted to feel pleasure rush over my body, maybe hoping one amazing orgasm with a man who I had feelings for, however misguided, would wash away the sea of hurt that had been my life.

He stood up abruptly. "I can't, Annie. I can't. It's not because I don't want to, because I do. I'd love to pleasure you. I care about you, and your son. Nothing good can come out of this. You need to heal and move on. This will only confuse you. I'm sorry."

He walked over to the bathroom and closed the door. I could hear the water run.

I knew he was doing what he thought was right. Trying not to hurt and damage me. But I deserved love. Would every man I ever developed feelings for be so afraid to hurt me that he would decide it was easier to walk away? Would I ever find love again? I hunched over in my chair, dejected and alone, again.

21. Patrick

THE STEAM FROM THE SHOWER fogged up the tiny mirror. I knew I was doing the right thing, no matter what my body was telling me. Annie couldn't possibly be ready to be intimate with a man after what she'd been through, especially a man who'd been one of her clients. I didn't want her to flash back to the brothel. She needed time for her body and her mind to recover, come to grips with what had happened to her.

I had to admit, I wasn't just thinking about her. I didn't have sex with women I knew or cared about. One-night stands, no strings attached, those were all I could handle. Could I make love to her and then walk away tomorrow?

I pulled on my clothes, and entered her bedroom. This entire voyage, I'd slept on the floor. Annie was curled in a ball on the bed. Her hair splayed around her head, her arms wrapped around her chest. She wore the simple cotton dress I'd picked out for her before I rescued her. The moonlight from the porthole illuminated her body. She was breathtaking.

The rest of the boat remained silent, except the gentle waves of the ocean rustling.

I climbed on the bed, wrapped my arms around her. She smiled, and turned to face me. Her body strained closer as I hovered over her, lowered my lips to hers. She opened her mouth slowly, hesitantly, and I forced myself not to be too enthusiastic. To go slow when I wanted to plunge my tongue into her mouth and take. Take it all. Take her.

Her lips attacked mine, a desperate kiss. I didn't resist. Her mouth was hot and wet. She didn't taste bitter and dry like I'd expected her to. No. She was salty and fruity, like a strawberry margarita. I had a fleeting desire to drink her up, taste every inch of her body, and pleasure her instead of forcing her to service me. I wanted to see a warm flush wash over her face and make her glow just for me. To make her come and scream out my name, and tell her she'd be safe and never scared again. I wanted to protect her and promise her as long as I lived, no man other than me would ever touch her again.

I couldn't allow myself to promise her anything, with words or my body. One kiss, it couldn't go beyond this one kiss. This kiss was the culmination of the nights I rocked her to sleep, prayed she would survive long enough for me to find her. We needed this kiss, one glimpse into what things might've been if we'd met under different circumstances.

I pulled away from her lips, and I felt like a magnet being pushed back toward her. But I was strong and I resisted. I turned her back around, spooning her. And like I had every night since I rescued her, I rocked her to sleep.

I could handle kissing her, but not waking up to her all sleepy and soft. She'd been wrapped around me like a vine, curled into my side with a leg thrown across my own, her breasts against my chest, and her face tucked into my neck. I tucked that feeling away, too, and pulled away from the embrace and the longing it stirred.

I wanted nothing more than to rouse her from sleep and kiss her more deeply than the night before, but that would lead us both down a road I wasn't sure I could come back from.

I was eating a pitiful excuse for a breakfast, runny, cold eggs and piss-poor coffee when she slipped into the galley kitchen in her meet-the-parents clothes, clutching Gabriel's hand. She was hesitant as she came closer; she looked almost hopeful.

The shame and regret twisted painfully in my chest when she smiled up at me, her cheeks flush with a burn from my beard. For the first time since I met her she seemed happy and it fucking pissed me off that I allowed myself to even get close to her and give her a false sense of hope.

"Hey, buddy. Did you have fun last night?"

He gave me a high five. "Fun last night." Gabriel had a habit of repeating what I said, which I found amusing.

Annie sat him down in a chair, and fidgeted with the hem of her dress as I made them breakfast.

"You ready?"

Confusion muddled her face and though I wanted to sidle up to her and tuck her into the comfort of my arm, I resisted. "Yeah, I have everything. How do I look?"

Her face glowed, as it had last night. All I wanted in that moment was to drag her back to our room and take back my promise not to make love to her. Instead, I frowned. "You look beautiful. Kyle, Vic, and I will wait outside your house and watch you walk in. Once I'm sure you're in safe hands, I'll go."

She blinked back tears, though I ignored them. I tried to pretend they were tears of excitement, but I could tell by her white pallor and tense stance that she was petrified.

She ate her breakfast in silence and I was both thankful and angry about every fucking thing. She finished and threw away the soggy paper plate; her shoulders slumped in defeat.

"Let's go."

I took both her and Gabriel's hands and led

them off the boat and dock. We'd docked at the SEAL base in Coronado so we wouldn't be hassled by customs and immigration. Vic and Kyle carried our luggage to Vic's Chevy Tahoe while Dave stayed behind on the boat. Annie, Gabriel, and I sat outside my office. Her eyes darted around, staring at the SEALs training on the beach. A few guys looked right at us and Annie's gaze lowered to the ground almost instantly. She tapped her foot and clutched my arm, almost leaving marks.

She turned to me. "About last night, I wanted to apologize—"

I cut her off. "Don't."

"Will you come see me when you return from deployment? I really would like to spend some time with you when you come back."

An image flashed in my mind of Annie and Gabriel greeting me on the dock after a deployment, holding a sign, and jumping up and down trying to get a better glimpse of me. "Annie, I don't think that's a good idea—for you or Gabriel. You need to heal and move on. We'll be bonded together forever because of this. But that's all there is. A memory. You're confusing your gratitude for your freedom with your feelings toward me. You don't know me. And I don't really know you, either. We have nothing in common. It was what it was. Now that you're back home, you'll get back with your rich, surfer boyfriend who keeps telling the press how much he misses you, and you'll forget I exist."

"That's impossible. And I doubt Chris has stayed faithful all these years. I'm sure he has a ton of girls. I'm not the same person I was when I left. No one has ever done anything for me like you have. I need you. I won't be able to forget you."

"Well, you're going to have to. I'm not the man you think I am."

Vic pulled the car around with Kyle in the passenger seat.

I opened the door for her and she squeezed inside, Gabriel sitting next to her in Vic's daughter's car seat. I sat next to Annie and held her hand. I didn't want to be a dick to her; I just didn't want to give her any hope there was a future for us. Because there wasn't.

As we drove away from the Navy base, my home, I looked out back at the yacht. I swallowed hard. After months of Annie consuming my thoughts, our time together was coming to an end.

Vic drove up the I-5 North. Annie was looking out the window at the coast.

"I never thought I'd see San Diego again." Annie had chills on her arms, and I put my arm around her to comfort her.

We exited in Encinitas, and Vic drove down to a street full of beachfront mansions. I knew she was loaded, but this place was ridiculous. Vic parked up the street from her house, and I helped her and Gabriel out of the car. Vic and Kyle both emerged to say good-bye.

"Thank you both for everything. I hope I'll see you guys again."

Vic gave her a hug. "Good luck, Annie."

Kyle also embraced her. "Of course we'll see you again. You're Pat's girl. I'm counting on hooking up with all your hottie friends."

Her mouth spread into a smile. "They'll love you."

I leveled Kyle with my eyes. I'd deal with him later.

"You guys stay here. I'll take her inside."

We walked up to the gate of her house, Annie holding on to my arm, Gabriel clutching my leg.

I bent over and gave Gabriel a hug. "Bye, little man. Take care of your mama for me."

He latched onto my neck, and I almost welled up with tears. "Bye, Pat."

I turned to Annie, her hair blowing in the ocean air. Would this be the last time I ever saw her? "Good-bye, Annie."

"Can't you come inside with me? Just for a bit?" I could feel Annie shake.

There couldn't be any ambiguity. I had to cut the ties. "No. You need to go by yourself. I'm not coming with you."

"But I need you. Please, I'm sure the Navy would give you leave? My daddy could get you a job and—"

My chest tightened. I fucking hated myself for

being such an asshole. I didn't have a choice—no one could find out about our involvement in her rescue. We'd gone over the cover story a bunch of times—Dave rescued her and sailed her home. I had to end this. For her. For me. For Gabriel. We both had to move on.

"Stop. We're not going to do this." My head pounded. I had to get it over with. Set her free so she could move on. "This is it, Annie. It's over. I can't ever see you again. I rescued you, and detoxed you. The job is done. This is done. I don't owe you anything. Just let it go."

Tears fell down her face and she let out a whimper.

I nudged Annie toward the gate, which she opened, then walked up to the front steps. Annie looked back at me, I nodded, and she rang the doorbell. Annie's mom, who I recognized from the pictures, opened the door, and let out a scream. She hugged Annie, Gabriel still standing by her side. I gave a final glance back and could see Annie's father appear at the door. Annie was safe. I'd done my job and completed my mission. It was time to get back to my men.

I raced up the street, jumped into Vic's SUV. "Go."

Vic sped away.

Maybe I shouldn't have been so harsh. I could've kissed her good-bye, told her it was going to be okay, and that I cared about her.

"You okay?" Vic offered.

"Yup. Never better," I lied.

I wondered what Annie was doing at that moment. Would her parents accept Gabriel? Like an investigative news reporter, I wanted to know every detail. But that was her story. My involvement in her life was over. Now it was time for me to get back to my life. I'd done my job, earned my trident.

The only easy day was yesterday.

22. Patrick

I WAS BACK ON THE USS Reagan, crammed next to my smelly men. In the week since I'd left Annie at her home, I'd thrown myself into work. Now, we were on our way to our next mission. During my week off, I completely unplugged: no phone, no Facebook, no internet. I hung out with my dog, went to a barbecue at Vic's house, and caught up on some movies. Normally, I'd log onto the computer every night, but I'd been avoiding the internet until now. Kyle and Vic had told me Annie's story had been all over the news, but I told them I didn't want to hear the details. One look at her in a news conference and I'd be stopping by her house to make sure she was okay.

Safely on the ship, I finally signed in once everyone else had dispersed so I could be alone. Against my better judgment, I googled her name.

"Missing American Analía 'Annie' Rose Hamilton Found Alive."

I scanned the article and nothing could've prepared me for what I read.

"Hamilton walked into her home in Encinitas, California. She has told authorities she ran away from the resort after a fight with her boyfriend and has been living in Aruba for the past five years under an assumed name as a missionary. She recently decided to return home and chartered a boat to San Diego."

What the fuck? No mention of being kidnapped, no mention of the brothel, no mention of Gabriel?

I took a deep breath and tried to come up with a reason, any reason, why Annie and her family would lie.

I found a video of a press conference on YouTube. It was a fucking circus: Annie, her parents, her boyfriend Chris, the police, lawyers, and the press. But again, no Gabriel. Where was he?

Annie didn't speak. She stood at the podium in a fitted, white suit, clutching the cheap necklace I'd given her.

Was she trying to send me a signal?

Her parents read from a prepared statement.

"We are so ecstatic to be reunited with our darling Annie. She is a testament to our faith in the Lord. Though we missed her all these years, we feel solace knowing she was doing God's work. To all the families with missing children out there, never give up hope. We ask for our privacy at this time as we rebuild our family."

Faith in the Lord? The Lord didn't find her, I did. I wasn't an atheist. I believed in God, I'd been raised Catholic. I hated the acceptance that everything which happened was part of God's plan. Was it God's plan for Annie to be kidnapped, forced to take drugs, and be raped every day?

Her boyfriend held her hand. I closed the website.

I found Kyle and Vic in the television lounge.

Kyle took one look at my face and grimaced. "So, you finally heard about Annie?"

"I don't understand why they'd lie. Where's Gabriel?"

Vic stood up. "She said her parents were pretentious assholes. What don't you get? They probably want to shield them from becoming tabloid superstars. 'Kidnapped sex slave and her son, fathered by her pimp, born in a brothel.' This is probably their way of protecting her."

I shook my head. "But they're lying. Like it or not, the dancer was his dad."

Kyle put his hand on my shoulders. "Pat, it's over. Just like you wanted. She kept our names out of the press. I'm sure Gabriel is fine. This way Annie can heal, get the help she needs to recover, without the media stalking her and her son. Knowing her awful story doesn't help anyone. Not her, not Gabriel. I talked to Dave—her parents gave him half of the reward, covered all of his expenses and then some, and he agreed to go along with their story."

I nodded my head. My gut told me something was wrong. Wrong with her family. Annie told me over and over that she was worried they wouldn't accept Gabriel. Had she been right? Were they embarrassed by him? Was this their way of trying to get Annie to detach from her child? Gabriel was such a cool, sweet boy. I hoped his grandparents were treating him right.

Six more months. Six more months and I'd be back in sunny San Diego. Less than twenty miles away from Annie. I'd told her I'd never wanted to see her again. I wasn't sure I'd meant it. For now, I had to focus on my next mission, get her crooked smile and her little boy's laughter out of my head.

23. Annie

THE BELL RANG AND JERKED me from my sleep. It had been months since I'd been in the brothel, but every bell, every whistle, and every wind chime spooked me.

This bell however was not for me to line up and greet johns. No, it was a meditation bell, at my so-called retreat, which was a fancy word for rehab. My parents had forced me to "get healthy" to deal with my trauma. I fucking hated every minute here. I missed my son, I missed Pat.

The grounds were beautiful. I was somewhere in Arizona, and my days consisted of yoga, massages, horseback riding, music therapy, group therapy, and individual therapy. Best that money could buy.

But of course I didn't participate in the group therapy—I was under strict orders by my family not to reveal what had happened to me to other patients. It was for my protection, they said. For Gabriel's. They didn't want him growing up knowing he was born in a brothel, that his father had been the one who had kidnapped and forced me into sex slavery. Gabriel was young, they said. He would forget about it. I was to rewrite history.

My psychiatrist knew the truth, the truth about everything, what had happened to me, Gabriel, the rescue, and my feelings toward Pat. She had signed a confidentiality agreement, and as a physician was bound to keep my secrets.

I should be grateful. I had my life back. I was free.

I didn't feel free. I felt trapped. Trapped in my mind.

Despite my counselor insisting to me over and over again that my feelings toward Pat were natural due to the fact he'd saved me, I knew in my heart she was wrong. I didn't love Pat because he saved me, though that clearly didn't hurt. I loved the way he looked at me as a woman, not as a victim. The way he played with my son. The way he held me at night. The way he kissed me, yet held back from going further. I felt his desire, I knew he wanted me.

And that kiss. What would it be like to kiss him every night, have him kiss every inch of my body, and have him bring me to the brink? Was I not allowed to have sexual thoughts because I was a recovering sex slave? I was so fucking sick of everyone telling me what I should feel: I should hate men and I should be so damaged that I should detest the touch of a man.

I wanted to be loved. I wanted to reclaim my sexuality. Enjoy sex, feel what it's like to experience pleasure from a man who loved me and wasn't using me. Didn't I deserve to be happy?

Pat said he wanted nothing to do with me. Did he mean it? Or was he just trying to protect me, afraid he could never give me what I needed.

I was due to check out of this place in a week. And I couldn't wait to be reunited with my son. Pat was deployed, I knew that. But I needed to see him again, and see if we had any chance of finding happiness together.

24. Patrick

TODAY WAS HOMECOMING. ALL THE other men would have their wives, girlfriends, and kids waiting for their arrival on the dock. Not me. I hadn't even bothered telling my mom when I'd be returning. No need for her to fly down from Northern California. I'd take leave soon and go visit her. For now, I wanted peace and quiet. Time to finally put all that had happened behind me.

Vic stopped by my rack. "Hey, man. What you doing Saturday? My family is having a fiesta for us—carne asada on the grill, tequila. You want to come?"

"Thanks, man. I'll text you. Tonight, I just want to get home to see my dog." Trigger had been staying with a SEAL buddy stuck on instructor duty, training BUD/S Phase One, for the wannabe SEALs.

"Okay. See you Saturday." He gave me a man-hug and headed out.

Despite my best intentions, I hadn't been able to resist keeping up with Annie's return. Luckily, my name hadn't been in the press and she had evaded revealing the details of her escape. She'd refused all interviews and her family had asked for privacy and time to heal. Of course, the internet had been rife with gossip—conspiracy theories, government cover ups, witness relocation. Maybe her choice to lie had been the correct one, because at least her and Gabriel's pictures weren't plastered all over the news.

I gathered my pack and gun. I couldn't wait to sleep in my own bed tonight.

Kyle and I walked down the gangplank after most of the sailors and Marines had dispersed. I wasn't in any rush. We were docked at the 32nd Street Naval Base. The beautiful view of the Hotel Del Coronado was behind me, and I marveled at the San Diego waterfront. I was happy to be home.

A sailor in front of me ran toward his wife, then cradled his infant, whom he was surely meeting for the first time. I couldn't imagine having to come home to this new life, new baby, and trying to make up for all the time I wasn't around. Being a stranger to my own family wasn't something that appealed to me.

Before I could scan the rest of the crowd, Kyle

whispered to me. "Your wife and kid are here."

My head turned. Annie stood before me, Gabriel at her side. She was holding a painted "Welcome Home Patrick!" sign. What the fuck were they doing here?

"Hey, Hero." She was stunning, and looked completely different than when I'd left her near her parents' house. Her black hair was blown dry and had lighter highlights framing her face. Her hazel eyes now seemed more golden, set off by her purple eye shadow. She'd gained some weight and her body looked soft and round—perfect. I couldn't take my eyes off the way her form-fitting pink sweater hugged her newly found curves. Curves which made my mouth dry. Gabriel was dressed in a little polo shirt and khaki pants. He beamed when he saw me and I scooped him up in my arms.

"Hey buddy!"

"Pat! Ship?" He pointed to the carrier. I wanted to give him a tour—but I didn't know where I stood with Annie.

Before I could greet Annie, Kyle was hugging her. I put Gabriel down and Kyle gave him a high five.

"You look gorgeous, Annie. I got to bounce but I'm sure I'll see you at Vic's barbeque Saturday?"

Dammit Kyle. Way to back me into a corner. I didn't know what Annie wanted from me or if she was visiting me out of gratitude or lingering feelings.

"I'd love to!"

"Great, see you then. Pat, I'll call you later."

Kyle winked and walked away, leaving me alone with Annie and Gabriel.

"How did you find me?"

Her hair blew in the wind and she smiled. "You're not the only one who can find people. My dad's was a Navy Lieutenant. He went to Annapolis."

Why hadn't she told me that before? Her dad was a ring knocker? Figured.

I wasn't ready to see her. I had planned on finding her before I deployed again, but on my terms. "What are you doing here? I told you we couldn't see each other—"

She bit her lip, her smile now sad. "Relax. I get it. Really . . . I just came to see you because I wanted to tell you thank you from the bottom of my heart. I'm sorry for the way I behaved detoxing and the last night on the ship. I clearly wasn't myself. Don't worry; I'm not going to stalk you."

Maybe I wanted her to stalk me. Fuck, I didn't know what the fuck I wanted. This new Annie wasn't the same beaten down girl I'd left behind. She was now strong, sexy, and confident, which only made me want her more.

The wind from the Pacific Ocean blew up her skirt, and I glimpsed black lace panties. I wanted to take her right there on the pier, hike up her skirt and fuck her brains out.

"Need a ride?"

Did I ever. Mind out of gutter. I'd planned on taking the shuttle back to the Naval Amphibious Base Coronado where my truck was parked. "I'm good. There's a shuttle."

She paused for a second. "Can I take you to lunch? Just to thank you. Then I'll leave you alone."

"I could eat." I followed her out to the parking lot. She pressed the button on her keys and a brand new deep purple Audi Q7 blinked its lights. "Nice ride."

"Oh, thanks. My dad bought it for me. I didn't want to drive anywhere by myself at first, but now I love it."

She put Gabriel in his car seat and I opened the driver's door for her. I came around to the passenger's side and slid in. This luxury SUV had all the bells and whistles—navigation, MP3, seat sensors.

She drove off base. My body remembered I hadn't been with anyone since her. But she wasn't my girlfriend picking me up after a long deployment and Gabriel wasn't my kid. We weren't a couple—I barely even knew her. We were just deeply connected by this experience. This was closure, for her and for me. And really, I was curious to see how she'd adjusted back to her old life. I wanted the truth, not lies fed from a tabloid. I needed to know she was okay and why she had lied. So I could move on and put her in the past. Finally.

There was something about her now which I couldn't figure out. A coolness. An air. She drove over the Coronado Bridge, down Coronado Avenue. Gabriel sang "Yo Gabba Gabba" songs. We pulled up to my favorite non-SEAL watering hole, Leroy's, and sat down at one of the reclaimed wood tables. I ordered a burger and a craft beer; she had ahi tacos and a lemon drop, Gabriel had a cheeseburger, fries, and chocolate milk.

"So, how you been? Any relapses?"

She rolled her eyes. "Good, I guess. No relapses. My parents sent me to a rehab-type emotional counseling place for a month. I hated it, to me it felt like being kidnapped all over again, and being away from Gabriel, but I guess it helped. I mean, nights are still no fun—I get scared and have nightmares. Plus, I find it hard to do anything without asking for permission."

So she was still waking up screaming at night, not from the detox but from nightmares. I wanted to be there for her, rock her to sleep.

"At least I'm healthy. I repeated all the tests Vic gave me. Luckily, no STDs. Even in the brothel, I always insisted on using a condom. Thank God prostitution was legal down there and I at least got tested. If the men refused to use one, I'd take the beating from my pimp rather than risk it. I always hoped one day I'd be able to escape."

I wanted to tell her she was lucky, but I couldn't

figure out a way to say it without sounding like I was vetting her for sex.

Gabriel was climbing around the seat, antsy. I took out my phone and let him play Angry Birds.

"Are you going back to school?"

She shrugged her shoulders. "Maybe. I don't know. I want to get into some kind of sex trafficking activism."

"That's great." Despite my desire to take her home with me, I kept my distance. She didn't need me dropping in and out of her life. I'd be leaving San Diego to train again in a month or so. "I saw your press conference. Why'd you lie?"

She bit her nails. "My parents thought it would be best, you know? Like my dad kept saying these people didn't need to know our business, we'd suffered enough. By you bringing me home, we had more options. I guess people see me as a selfish brat who left her family, but isn't that better than being seen as a sex slave?"

"I guess, Annie. Your call. But what about Gabriel? You don't think he'll remember? Does anyone know the truth?"

"I hope not. He's so young. My parents have told everyone I was married to a missionary, we had Gabriel, and then his father was killed."

I shook my head. "The more lies you tell, the harder it gets. Trust me. Someone will find out the truth."

She shrugged. "I didn't really have a choice, Pat.

I can't really work right now, I'm jumpy. And I need to take care of Gabriel. My parents financially support me. I had to go along with what they wanted. Chris knows, he had a right to because he was blamed for my disappearance, but he's the only one, and my therapist. Maybe one day I'll tell my story."

I sighed. This wasn't how I'd wanted her life to go, not that I had a say. I'd pictured her becoming strong and independent, hailed as a survivor. Now she still seemed to have little control over her life.

She reached across the table and touched my hand. My body craved her caress. "I need another favor."

Why the hell not? It'd been months. I grinned and squeezed her hand. "Let's go. I'll take you back to my place."

She blushed. "No, no, not that. I'm sorry I begged you that night. When I'm finally ready to be with a man I want it to be special, to mean something. Know that he loves me."

It would be special and mean something to me. I couldn't put my feelings about her into words. "What do you want?"

"Um, so, you can say no. But my dad wants to meet you and personally thank you for saving me."

Fuck no. I clenched my fist. "Not going to happen, Annie. I assume you already told him how we met? Hi, sir. Well, yes, I visited a whorehouse in

Aruba and hired your daughter to give me a blowjob. No way."

"It's important to him to meet you."

"Sorry, Annie. But the answer is no."

"Please. Just this once then I'll leave you alone. I promise. He just really wants to thank you."

"You're not going to leave me alone until I agree?"

"Pretty much."

"No, Annie. I can't. I'm sorry."

"Fine. Forget I asked." She bit her nails, and rummaged through her purse. "I'll leave you alone. I can take you back to base now."

I wasn't about to meet her family, but I wasn't ready to say good-bye. "Do you and Gabriel want to come to Vic's party?"

Her eyes beamed. "We'd love to. I wasn't sure you really wanted me to go. It's tomorrow, right?"

"No, Saturday. I'll pick you up at five. At the coffee house down the street from your house?" I wasn't just being a dick, not picking them up from her house; I really didn't want her family to see my face. I still didn't trust, despite their cover up, that I'd somehow pulled off this rescue without getting caught.

"Sounds good. I can't wait."

We finished our meals and went to Bay Books next door. I bought Gabriel a counting book about the Navy. Then we grabbed ice cream. Had I been wrong about being incapable of taking care of anyone other than myself? I thought seeing her back in the United States, free, would squelch any feelings I had for her, protecting her, loving her. She didn't seem happy to me, truly happy. And I had some crazy notion I could make her happy again. That, in some twisted way, our fucked up past could make each other whole.

25. Annie

MY HAND TREMBLED AS I twisted up one more coat of mascara onto my eyelashes. Since I'd been back home, I almost never put on makeup. It reminded me of being at the brothel. But I wanted to look nice for Pat. I was meeting him in a half an hour. Was this a date? It felt like a date, whatever I imagined a date would feel like. I wouldn't really know—Chris and I just fell into a relationship in high school. He even recently confessed to me that he was planning on proposing on our last night on the vacation. I still loved him, I would always love him—he was my first, the only man I'd been with until I was taken. But there was too much pain and sadness between us. The guilt of what had happened to me wrecked him. He blamed himself, if only he'd awoken, or we hadn't been drunk, he was sure that he could've prevented my kidnapping. I didn't blame him, at all. But we had nothing left. Years of wondering, suspicion, longing had squashed any chances of us finding happiness.

But with Pat it was different. I felt different. He was so sexy, beautiful, deep. Loyal and committed. His strong arms, sexy mouth, my mind ran wild imagining him making love to me. Though I knew he felt guilt for hiring me, I knew in his fucked up mind he felt that hiring a hooker was safe for him emotionally. No promises. No disappointments. But he could never disappoint me.

I walked out of my bathroom, and into the family room, where my parents were watching television, Gabriel playing quietly on the floor.

My father gave me a hard glance. "You look nice. Date with Chris?"

His voice was almost hopeful. His sad blue eyes broke my heart. I knew it just killed him to see me, imagine what I'd been through. And Gabriel was just a reminder to him of my ordeal, despite how hard he tried to love him. My father couldn't even look at Gabriel. Daddy's little girl died on that vacation. "No, Dad. We're meeting Pat. He's taking us to a barbeque with the other guys who saved us."

He let out a pained breath. "You're meeting him? He doesn't even have the decency to pick you up at your home and meet me?"

"Dad, stop. It's not like that. He's embarrassed

about how we met. If I continue to see him, you'll meet him. He's a good guy, I swear."

He pointed at me. "He's a good SEAL, Annie. Don't confuse his job proficiency with his character. Remember where you met him, how he hired you for his selfish needs. No morals. No ethics. I'm surprised he made it through BUD/S. He's not the type of man you want around your son."

"Well, he's a helluva improvement from Gabriel's real dad." That ought to shut him up.

My dad just shook his head and walked away. My parents' constant newfound concern for and control over me irked me to no end. What were they trying to protect me from? I'd already lived the worst life imaginable.

I brushed Gabriel's hair, put on his shoes, and we walked out of our door, toward the coffee house. Toward Pat. I was so nervous. Seeing him two days ago had brought back all the feelings I'd had on the ship. It was real—not just some misplaced affection for my savior. He cared about me, and Gabriel. He'd seen me at my worst. Yet he looked at me with desire, not disgust. Not as some used up heroin addicted whore, but as a woman, as a mother. A survivor.

I wanted him. I wanted to make him feel love, make him trust me. I would never cheat on him. If he would only give me a chance. Give us each a chance to build a new life together. Based on truth. How could I ever be with anyone who didn't understand and accept my former life? Star is a part of me. I don't want to forget her. The kidnapping happened. I was a sex slave. That is my past—but I won't let it define my future.

26. Patrick

I ARRIVED AT LOFTY COFFEE twenty minutes early. I didn't want to be late. My stomach was in knots—this felt like going on a first date, and I didn't date. Annie still hadn't arrived, so I slipped out the door to The Den, a boutique next store. I wanted to buy her something.

The designer clothes and lingerie weren't what I was looking for. Then something caught my eye at the counter. "I'll take this."

The shop girl grabbed the item and packaged it up. "Is this for your girlfriend?"

I couldn't tell if she was hitting on me, but I didn't care. "Something like that."

I paid, and went back to the coffee shop.

Annie had arrived but hadn't noticed me yet. She and Gabriel were standing in line.

I couldn't resist checking her out. She was wearing a pale peach dress that clung to her body. I couldn't tell if she had a bra on or one of those camisoles. Either way, I could see the outline of her nipples. I clenched my fists and tried to reconcile this beautiful woman standing in front of me with the traumatized hooker I'd first laid eyes on. A mixture of shame for how I met her with pride at how she'd recovered filled my mind.

I leaned into her and kissed her, not caring about my own objections. The words spilled out of my mouth, the look on her face made me happy as I said them. "I'm glad you came to greet me off the ship. Honestly, I haven't been able to stop thinking about you."

She touched my face, her fingers tracing my beard. "I missed you, too."

We ordered two cold-drip iced coffees and chocolate milk for Gabriel.

Annie was turned toward the coffee bar adding milk and sugar to our drinks. Some dickhead handed her the plastic covers and said something to her to make her blush. I wanted to punch him.

She handed me my coffee. Her cheeks were red.

I put my arm around her, grabbed Gabriel's hand, and headed back to my truck.

I texted Vic and told him we were on our way. I really wanted to see how she would act around the other Team guys and their wives. I wasn't trying to test her, yet I couldn't help but be curious if there was any possibility she'd ever fit into my world. I mean, I was still going to ship out and be away from her again, without a doubt. But it was like there was a part of me that wanted to know for sure, wanted to see how stupid any vague lingering idea of us.... No. This could never work, no matter how much we might both want it. I'd used her once; I was one of her johns. And despite her claiming she was better, she was probably too emotionally damaged to be in a relationship.

God, she looked hot in her dress.

Forty minutes later, we arrived at Vic's family's house. The smell of cumin and lime wafted from the backyard.

I didn't need to knock. We walked around the back and opened the gate.

About twenty other Team guys, plus their wives and kids, were milling around the yard. There was one of those bouncy houses for the kids. Gabriel's eyes widened. I wasn't sure if he was used to kid centric parties; somehow I doubted Annie's parents had fully embraced him, but I honestly didn't have a clue.

Vic spotted us. He poked Kyle to get his attention and they both came over.

"Annie! You look great." Vic hugged her. "Thanks for coming."

A hug wouldn't satisfy Kyle. "Hey, sweetheart!" He lifted her in the air. She seemed more excited to see him than she had to see me. Not that I had anything to worry about—we never ever hit on another Team guy's woman. "How've you been? Where are all the hottie friends you promised me?"

She smiled. "I'll hook you up."

Vic's mother walked over to us, his daughter Carina trailing behind her.

"Mama, this is Annie and her son Gabriel," Vic told her.

"Hola, mija. Bienvenida." I loved Vic's mom; she was like a second mother to me. She never hesitated to make food for an entire SEAL Team or drive downtown in the middle of the night to pick one of us up if we were smashed.

"Encantada, Señora Gonzales. Soy Analía."

Vic's mom seemed impressed by Annie's fluent Spanish. Three-year-old Carina looked up at Annie and then back at Gabriel. Vic's little princess was adorable—huge brown eyes, long wavy hair tied up in a bow. I admired how he made her his top priority when he was in town, knowing that as long as he remained in the Teams, they would spend more time apart than together.

"You wanna see my dolls?" Carina asked Gabriel.

Gabriel nodded.

Carina led Gabriel into the house, and Vic's mom went to the kitchen.

Our Teammate Joe's wife Tori walked over, carrying a tray of beers. Tori was a SEALs dream woman. Gorgeous, great mom, faithful. They'd been high school sweethearts. Joe had just been selected for SEAL Team Six, our most elite Team and was currently deployed. No doubt, his success was directly attributed to the love and support of his wife.

"Annie, this is Tori. Her husband Joe is one of my best friends. He's deployed."

Tori reached out her hand. "Hi, Annie. Nice to meet you. How did you meet Pat?"

Annie pulled on her hair, her face now white.

Fuck, we hadn't prepared for questions. I was about to open my mouth, but Annie started talking.

"Pat picked me out of a line-up . . . . at a country bar and asked me to dance, said I was the prettiest girl there."

I spit out my beer. "Annie was the most beautiful girl that night for sure, but she's also a champion soccer star and a great mom. I fell for her the moment I met her." I winked at Annie.

"Well, you must be pretty special, Annie. Pat never brings anyone around us. Ever. I've known him for eight years. He's a good guy, saved my husband's life. Why don't you come over and I'll introduce you to the other wives."

Annie looked up at me, as if asking for permission. I squeezed her hand and she and Tori walked over to the other women.

Kyle gave me a devilish grin. "Couldn't stay away from her for a day. We've been back, what, five hours? Have you already hit that?"

"Two days, asshole. You saw her greet me at the

dock. Welcome home sign and everything."

Vic raised his eyebrow. "What's the problem? You wanted to see her anyway."

I glanced over near the pool; Annie was sitting at a table chatting with the other women. She gave me a big smile and waved at me. "Yeah, I did. But, I mean, she has Gabriel, and we'll leave again soon. I don't want to confuse him; poor kid's been through enough."

Vic jumped in. "Walsh, she wants you. She's a good girl. And she's gorgeous. You have nothing to lose. Stop being such a closed-off prick and give her a chance."

I was going to respond, but Annie walked over to me carrying a plate of food.

She smiled and I couldn't help but think even though I didn't fit in her life, she sure seemed at home in mine.

27. Patrick

AFTER A FEW HOURS AT the party, I was about to leave and take Annie and Gabriel home. Carina had worn Gabriel out playing house, and the little guy was passed out on the floor.

Vic's mom whispered. *"Pobrecito, mijo."*

"Why don't you and Annie go somewhere? Let Gabriel sleep. If he wakes while you're gone, I can keep him entertained," Vic offered.

"Oh. I don't know. Are you sure that's okay?" Annie crinkled her brow.

"Yeah, I'll just be cleaning up. We'll be fine."

"Okay. But we'll only be gone for an hour."

"Don't worry about it—take your time."

I was excited and nervous to get alone time with Annie. I didn't even know where to take her. I decided I'd show her around the SEAL base, since it was close by the back roads. It was private, beautiful, and where I spent the majority of my life. As we drove in my beat-up black truck from Chula Vista through Imperial Beach on our way to Coronado, I couldn't shake the gnawing feeling that I shouldn't push her away. I'd been alone for so long, I didn't even know what my life would be like with a girlfriend.

The view of the Silver Strand beach was on our left and Annie stared out the window.

"You okay?"

She blinked back tears. "Yup."

I touched her thighs, sliding my hand in between them. Not to start anything, just to touch her. It would take me a lifetime to comprehend what she'd been through.

"Tell me."

"It's nothing."

"I want to know."

Her hands shook. "I was having fun at the party, just being normal. Everyone was so nice to me. But I kept thinking they were all looking at me. No one brought up the fact I've been on the cover of every magazine, flashed across all the news networks. I haven't been out in public much. Everyone must think I'm this bitch who abandoned her family and let her boyfriend become a suspect for murder, just to run off."

I had no idea she'd felt everyone was judging her. "First, none of that is true. If you want to ever want to tell anyone what really happened to you, I support you. Any of them who recognized you probably think you had a good reason to vanish and were in awe of your strength. And all the other Team guys were jealous I had the hottest girl there."

"Thanks, Pat. You're full of shit, but I appreciate your effort."

We pulled in to the Naval Amphibious base, and I decided to give her a quick tour. When I showed her the obstacle course, her eyes got wide. "I want to try it."

"Who are you, GI Jane?"

"I could do it. I don't quit."

Totally off limits to chicks, I stared at the course. Some of my toughest memories were climbing a rope, carrying logs over my head, maneuvering under barbed wire, and scaling walls. I didn't think women should ever be allowed to train as SEALs. Call me a misogynist asshole, but why can't men just be men? Like, we couldn't even have porn anymore because we couldn't risk offending women. Fuck that. But the thought of seeing Annie, dirty and sweating, writhing on the ground, and begging me for mercy, made me willing to make an exception.

"Maybe someday I'll let you try. If you're a good girl." I wanted to smack her tight little ass, but I didn't want to disrespect her. I imagined taking her from behind, dominating her, making her scream my name. But after what she had been through, I was also worried about scaring her. Any sexual experience with her had to be slow, sensitive, and all about her.

We found a secluded spot on the beach. Most of the tourists had deserted by then and we were blessedly alone, shrouded by the trees and warmed by the remnants of the sun. As the sun began to set, I threw a blanket down, pulled Annie on it, and wrapped her in my arms. Whatever this was, she felt right there, like she belonged. Her hair smelled like vanilla, and it drove me wild remembering the night I had her wrapped around me.

"You know, I never was a beach bunny. Chris surfed, and my girlfriends spent all their time down here sunbathing, but it was never my thing. Once I was taken, though, every time I had a chance to look outside, I would try to see the ocean. It meant freedom to me. A way off the island."

"I actually hate the ocean. You'd think as SEALs, most of us would love it. But after going through Hell Week, spending all that time training while being wet and sandy, the last thing we want to do is spend our free time near the beach."

She squeezed my knee and smiled slowly. "I'd love to see you wet and sandy."

Grrr. I wanted to make her wet, but not from the ocean. From my mouth, from my hands, from my cock.

"Tori seemed nice."

"Yup. She's amazing. Great woman. Joe lucked out."

"You saved him?"

I paused. I never talked about my missions with anyone, other than fellow SEALs. But I trusted Annie. Completely. "Yeah. Two years ago, we were in Afghanistan. We were deep undercover. I'd made the call to let some unarmed Afghani civilians go, which is protocol. But we were ambushed. We lost a few men, good men. Joe was wounded, but I dragged him to safety."

Her hand glided along my shoulder, a soft comforting touch. She didn't say anything, she didn't need to. Normally, I would push away any form of sympathy; my machismo thought that expressing my feelings made me weak. But I liked being vulnerable with Annie. I'd seen her at her worst; she could see me at mine.

I reached into my pocket and took out a small box. I shoved it in her hands. "Here. I got this for you, to replace the shitty one I bought you in Aruba."

She opened the box and pulled out a tiny necklace. It was a small, gold trident. Our symbol. My code.

"I love it! Thank you, Pat." She turned her back to me and I unhooked the necklace I'd given her.

"Wait. Stop. I want to wear that one also."

"Why? It's cheap. Cost me fifty cents."

She clutched the old necklace to her chest and the sight caused me to feel oddly protective. "But it's worth fifty thousand dollars to me. It gave me hope. Hope that you would return and save me."

I hooked it back on and placed the other one around her neck. "I've never met anyone like you. You're so resilient."

"I couldn't give up. I had to give Gabriel a chance at a future."

I took her hand. "I leave again in six weeks. For three months. After that, I'm not sure how long I'll be back here until our next mission."

"I don't care, Pat. One thing I learned in captivity was to not focus on the future or the past. Just take one day at a time. I'm happy with you today. We don't need to plan out the rest of our lives. As long as you want to be with me now, that's enough for me. I waited for five years for someone to save me. I'd wait another five years for you to come back home to me. I'd never cheat on you—"

"I know you wouldn't cheat—I wasn't worried about that. It's more complicated. I'll never see you." I needed her to really get what life being with me would be like. There was no happily ever after in store for us. Longing, heartache, loneliness. That was all I could provide.

"I can't connect with anyone back home. My parents, my friends, Chris. It's so crazy. Everyone expects me to be who I was before I left—like I can just slip back into my old life. But I'm not the same person. And I'm also not some careless girl who ran away for five years. I'm a woman. I want to fall in love. I want to take control over my body. I want to feel pleasure. Those men took five years of my life and I won't allow them to take a second more. Being kidnapped was something horrible that happened to me, but I refuse to make it define me. And I have the greatest gift from that experience. Gabriel. I hate to be a bitch, but I hear my friends whining about stupid stuff, like not having enough money for new clothes, or their boyfriends spending too much time with their friends. Who gives a fuck? I mean, I was raped every day for five years. I'm a recovering heroin addict. That will be a part of who I am for the rest of my life."

I shook my head; she had to listen to me. "I hear what you're saying, but I can't give you what you need. As much as I want to. You will always be lonely. There will be days, weeks where you won't know if I'm alive or dead. And you have Gabriel. He needs a constant presence in his life."

"I'd never be lonely with you. You are here in my heart. I'm trying to tell you that with you, I don't have to explain myself, apologize for what happened, or lie about the past. You know what I've been through, and you're still here. You don't see me as a victim. You see my strength."

"I don't want you to be anything other than what feels right to you, Annie. You're perfect just the way you are and no one or nothing can change that. You proved that by surviving."

She was angled in my lap with her legs thrown over mine, her head resting against my chest and in that moment I realized I didn't want whatever it was between us to end. I wasn't ready to call it love. All I knew was I wasn't ready to let her go.

"That means a lot to me. I hate lying to everyone and even my parents act awkward whenever I'm around. My dad won't even look at Gabriel. You're the only one who seems to treat me like a person."

The breeze coming off the water surrounded us with the salty sea air, like a warm cocoon. With the lock of her gaze on mine, the rest of the world seemed to fade away and it was just us, wrapped in each other. "I want to make this work."

She pulled out of my arms and her brows creased. "You do?"

It had just slipped out, but the more that I thought about it; the more I was growing to like the idea. The time without her those first few months had been hell and the more I was around her, the more I wanted to throw caution to the wind.

"I'm serious." I pushed a lock of hair off her forehead, tucked it behind her ear. "I know I said I didn't want for us to take this any farther than the boat, but apparently nothing stops you, which I admire more than anything. I do enjoy spending time with you and Gabriel. I want you." I moved my lips just a hairsbreadth from hers and I felt her deep inhalation at my declaration.

She smiled and her delicate hand drew up to press against my cheek in a soft caress. "I couldn't imagine being with anyone else. I don't know how or where this is going to go, but I haven't been able to stop thinking of you. You're the only one I feel comfortable with."

I pressed my lips to hers. I poured every ounce of pent up lust and frustration into the kiss. My hand on her waist crushed her to me, the other tilting her head to the side to take the kiss deeper.

Her hand shifted into my hair to hold me against her and the kiss turned emotional, softer, more loving.

The fabric of the dress she wore billowed out around us, concealing the motion, though the beach was pretty much deserted. I shifted, sliding my hands down the slope and dip of her hips and wrapped around to grab her tight ass. I clenched and gripped to guide her movements, pressing her more firmly against me with each slide.

I wanted to take her then and there, connect with her completely. I hadn't had sex in a year and even then it was a one-night stand before I left for deployment and met Annie. I didn't even remember the girl's name. Jamie? Janie? But I had a feeling a year from now, ten years from now, I would remember this moment, just as I could recall our kiss on the boat. There was something about this girl, the way she focused on me, and saw right through me.

And that's exactly why I stopped. My hands dropped and my lips detached from hers.

"Don't stop, Pat. I want you."

"Hey, I'm right here, babe. I'm dying to be with you, but not like this. I want it to be perfect, romantic. Not on some beach. There's no rush. I'm not going anywhere."

"Relax, I'm not a virgin. We don't have to wait."

I didn't laugh. "It's not just about you. I told you; I was raised by a single mom. I refuse to pop in and out of Gabriel's life, anymore than I have to because of my job. We just started dating. I'm not going to make love to you until I can commit to you and Gabriel. Once I commit, I do it one hundred percent. If we are going to make this work, we need to base this relationship on something other than the fucked up way we met."

She threw her arms around my neck. "That's the sweetest thing I ever heard."

I kissed her again. It was like a relationship in reverse. She'd sucked my dick before I even knew her name. I only had one choice now. Go slow. So slow it would hurt. "Let's go. Just in case Gabriel wakes up."

She stood up, dusted the sand off her dress, and we walked back to my truck. It was late and I had to pick up Gabriel and take them both back to her home. And I knew now I wouldn't be able to put off meeting her parents much longer.

28. Patrick

I'D PROMISED ANNIE I WOULD finally meet her parents now that we were together. I drove my rusted truck up the I-5 North toward Annie's parents' home in Encinitas. The damn truck still ran, thanks to my buddies taking care of it. With all the money I'd saved up during deployment, I briefly considered upgrading it to a brand new Ford Raptor. I needed to put down some roots, maybe buy a condo. But in this real estate market, the chances of doing that were slim.

I arrived at Annie's house, and I flashed back to dropping her off here six months ago. She'd been so scared, so hopeful. She'd already come so far.

The grand gate opened and I pulled into their driveway. It was sad that with all the resources her parents had, they hadn't been able to find Annie. Just hire former SEALs to bring her back home—

real SEALs, not some asshole pretenders. But Dave said he'd seen some guys looking for Annie—who were they? I knew a few security contracting firms filled with former Team guys who could've gotten the job done. I'd sell every possession I owned to save my daughter. Give my life.

I glanced in the car mirror. I wore a collared shirt and khaki pants. I'd even shaved. I looked like a preppy asshole—should fit right in.

Annie came around to the side of my truck, carrying Gabriel. I recognized her parents immediately from all the news coverage. Her father had a distinguished white beard and piercing blue eyes. Her mother looked like one of those reality television housewives—long, shiny black hair, almond-shaped chocolate eyes, and porcelain skin.

I removed my sunglasses and stepped out of the truck. Her father observed me coolly, and offered a hand, which I took. "It's an honor to meet you, Patrick."

Her mother gave me a quick hug. Tears shone in her eyes as she looked up at me. "Thank you for saving my baby."

"You're welcome. I didn't do it alone."

"Yes, but you risked your life and career for her." Her mom hugged me again and I could smell her strong perfume. "You brought our Annie back home."

"Okay, Mom, can we at least go inside before

you start losing it?"

"Of course, baby."

I followed Annie up to the elegant entry stairs. The view of Moonlight State Beach from the living room blew me away. This home had to be worth at least three million dollars. I felt more at home in the brothel than I felt in this palace.

Her father stood in front of the bar. "So, Patrick. Can I get you something to drink? A martini perhaps?"

Who did they think I was—James Bond? What twenty-five-year-old guy drinks martinis? I grunted. "Thank you, sir. That sounds great." Fuck. I didn't even know how to talk to these people.

I studied Annie as she sat with her back erect on the white leather sofa and bit her nails. This was her home, but she didn't seem comfortable. And it sure as hell wasn't kid friendly for Gabriel. Sharp-edged glass table, ceramic vases. Couldn't they hire someone to child proof now that they had their grandson living here?

This place was so pristine, like a museum. If her parents had seen where she had been living for the past five years, they would've had heart attacks. Well, at least with their cover story, no tabloid would return to Aruba and try to retrace Annie's steps, expose what had happened to her. The brothel burnt down, so even if they ever went back her parents wouldn't know how bad her existence truly had been.

But I would never forget. The smells of sex, drugs, sweat, and smoke were permanently ingrained in my head.

When I looked up, I met her father's glare. He'd returned a few moments prior and by the narrowing of his eyes he must have seen me watching her. Great.

Her father handed me the martini, his cold eyes assessing. "Can I have a word with you on the deck?"

The martini even came with the standard-issue blue cheese stuffed olive. Bonus. I took a sip of the liquor. I suddenly had a feeling I would probably need all the alcohol I could get.

"Sure, sir." I followed him out to the redwood deck. I'd rather be interrogating a terrorist than be alone with this former Naval Officer. I downed the rest of the martini.

I breathed in the salty ocean air. I would never own a house like this. My own one bedroom rental could fit in the size of their living room.

"So, Patrick. Annie told me everything. How you met, how you rescued her. I'd like to thank you for your service."

My service? "It was the right thing to do."

He reached into his pocket and placed a folded piece of paper in my hand. "This should cover your expenses."

I opened it. It was a three hundred thousand

dollar check made out to Patrick Walsh. I'd be able to help my mom out, buy a new truck, and put a down payment on a condo. Pay off debt. I could live a fairly comfortable life for years on the amount of money I held in the palm of my hand.

I didn't hesitate to hand it back to him. "I can't accept this."

Mr. Hamilton laughed; his nose lifted in disgust, and shoved the check back into my hand. "Yes, you can. I knew men like you in the Navy—pieces of shit who would cheat on their wives with hookers. I hope you can leave us alone to heal. In private." His eyebrow rose. "Annie has been through enough. Seeing you is a reminder of her past. How you used her, forced her to get you off. I don't want scum like you hanging around my daughter."

My own vision narrowed, I opened my stance and took a few controlling breaths. Who the fuck did this guy think he was? "I can't be bought off. If it wasn't for me, Annie would still be shooting up heroin and screwing strangers. Or dead. You think I'm scum?" I sneered. "You should've seen her pimp." I ripped up the check, went back inside, and charged toward the front door.

No one was going to tell me how to live my life and who I could see.

Annie was waiting in the dining room, her mother close by her side. Their heads both shot in my direction as I strode through the perfectly appointed kitchen and then past them. I ignored the smirk on her mother's face and the frown on Annie's.

"Are you leaving?" she called after me. "We haven't even eaten yet."

If I left, I'd be doing exactly what her father wanted. He wasn't going to win. I wanted to be with Annie and no one was going to stop me.

"No. I just need a second."

"Okay, do you want a tour?"

"Sure."

I took the stairs behind her two at a time and followed her into a room, where she sat down on the bed; her shoulders hunched inward, hands lying limply on her lap.

"This is my bedroom," she whispered.

I glanced around the room. Its stark white walls had weird pictures of Victorian children in frames above the sleigh bed, and tiny little porcelain dolls arranged on an antique vanity. It reeked of a combination of mothballs and potpourri. "Your room? Are you eighty? This place is creepy. You actually sleep in here? No wonder you have nightmares."

She gave me a dazed expression. The same one I had seen back on the boat. "Well, my mom had it redecorated after I went missing—used it as a guest room. I understand, I guess. They had me declared legally dead. For insurance and stuff. I don't see the point in redecorating it. I'm going to move out at some point. I don't really feel comfortable here."

"How do you not feel comfortable in your own home? Didn't you grow up here?"

"Yes." She stroked the flowery bedspread. "But it feels so different now. All traces of me had been removed. I don't blame them for moving on."

What the fuck was wrong with her family? I didn't understand rich people. My mom worked two jobs to support me. She still lived in the same crappy thirteen hundred square foot house I grew up in back in Sacramento. Even when I brought my ex-fiancée back home to meet her, she hadn't changed one thing about my room. Hadn't Annie's parents wanted something to remember her by when they thought they'd lost her forever?

"Can I see Gabriel's room?"

"He...he doesn't have a room. He sleeps in here. I like him close."

"Are you serious? This place is huge and he doesn't have his own space? Where does he put all his toys?"

"We play outside, and in the basement. He doesn't have too much stuff."

I swallowed around the knot in my throat. I couldn't believe what I was about to do. "Why don't you and Gabriel move in with me?"

"What? I thought you wanted to take things slow."

I took a step closer so my knees bumped hers. I lifted her chin with the tips of my fingers. "I do. Physically. But I want you around me all the time and I love that little boy. He can put his trains and toys all over my place."

"Maybe. I don't know. I don't want to impose. I haven't even seen your place yet."

"That's fair. Tomorrow you guys come by and I'll make you dinner."

"What about dinner here, tonight?"

"I'm sorry, Annie. I tried, but I really don't feel comfortable here." I wanted to tell her what her father had said to me, but my desire to protect her made me keep it to myself.

"Okay. I'll walk you out."

I followed her down the stairs to the entryway. Her parents hovered behind her; Gabriel sat in the corner, seemingly hypnotized by an iPad. Her mother's face was Botox-tense and the smile she wore was more of a sneer. I resisted the urge to roll my eyes and instead turned to pull Annie in a hug. They shared a look which I caught from over Annie's head. Fuck them. I didn't need their approval. If anything, they should want their daughter to be happy considering what she'd been through.

We bypassed her parents and went down the hallway, out into the yard, and back down to the driveway. I looked up at the expansive glass windows, and could see her dad watching me. I wasn't intimidated by him. He wanted to watch? I'd give him something to watch. I pulled Annie to me, cupped her face, kissed her lips. She was mine, and

I wasn't going to hide our relationship from anyone. She'd spent enough of her life hiding.

A moment passed and I just stared at Annie. Even though we'd only known each other for a short time, there was an ease and comfort level between us that I'd never experienced with anyone. "I'll pick you up at five."

"Sounds good."

I slid into my truck and drove away.

It wasn't just that her family was loaded; I couldn't shake the feeling something wasn't right with her family. And I was going to find out what it was. For Annie's sake.

29. Patrick

THE NEXT DAY, WE DROVE in silence to my tiny one-bedroom apartment in Pacific Beach. It wasn't much to look at, but it had a small courtyard for Trigger and was close to all the shops and restaurants.

I showed Annie and Gabriel my medals in my apartment. Gabriel was happy to play with a toy SEAL boat I'd bought for him. Annie seemed impressed and asked a ton of questions about my job. I was touched that she seemed to really care about my career, more so than the typical girl. Most Frog Hogs saw us as nothing more than a notch on their bedposts, a real life hero from one of those sappy romance novels. The SEALs in those books had little resemblance to real Team guys. First off, most SEALs never ever told people what we did for a living. I would've never told Annie I was a SEAL, but I needed to make her understand I was capable of saving her. I always told everyone I met that I worked at the airport in baggage claim. Another thing, we never gave details about our missions to civilians, whether we were fucking them or not. And we sure as hell didn't leave our careers to chase women across the world. Most of the authors who wrote that crap had never even met a SEAL, let alone been fucked by one.

I cooked them dinner, nothing fancy just spaghetti and a salad. Gabriel wouldn't touch the spaghetti but he was happy eating crackers. I enjoyed taking care of them.

Annie reached for her phone. "I have to call home. They'll worry."

"Worry about what? You're with me."

"After what happened, they freak if I stay too long at yoga." She picked up her cell phone and dialed.

"Hi, Dad... We're good."

She shifted her phone to her right ear, probably so I couldn't hear her dad tell her what a piece of shit I was.

"Whatever, Dad. I gotta go."

She ended the call and looked out the window.

"You okay?"

"Yeah."

I knew her dad must've given her a hard time. "What did he say?"

"That you were just a typical SEAL who was going to leave me and cheat on me. 'Remember where you met him, Annie. That's not the kind of man you want to get involved with or the type of role model you want for your son.' Whatever, I don't care. They'll get over it. They can't really pretend to try to protect me from anything. I've already survived the worst life imaginable."

"My offer stands, you both can stay here."

She reached up and kissed me. "I'd like that."

We popped in a movie for Gabriel, Turbo. He eventually fell asleep in front of the television.

I opened the door and leashed up Trigger for a quick walk. "I'll be right back."

"Can I take a shower?"

I was tempted to jump in with her and see the beads of water glisten off her body. "Make yourself at home."

Trigger was grateful to spend time with me. Some would say it was stupid to get a dog when I was deployed so much. But Trigger was my family. His loyalty was boundless.

We entered the courtyard and Trigger sniffed a tree. I took my phone out and saw I'd had missed a call from Kyle. I called him back and he picked up on the first ring.

"Hello?" his voice sounded groggy.

"Hey, man. Sorry I missed your call. Annie and Gabriel are here."

"How's it going?"

"Yesterday I met her family. Her dad tried to bribe me to stay away from her."

"What an asshole. You said no, right?"

"Of course I did. But that's not it. There's something going on with her parents."

Kyle's voice deepened. "Keep talking."

"I don't have anything yet, but something doesn't add up. I mean, I found her and I wasn't even looking. And Dave mentioned those contractors were looking for her. You'd think with all that money they could find her?"

"I thought they also hired some guy who took their money?" Kyle said.

"That's what the news stories say, but her dad's a former Naval Officer—he couldn't check out this guy's credentials before giving him three hundred thousand dollars?"

"You're right. That makes no sense," Kyle said.

I nodded. "I'm going to put some calls in with some friends who work in security contracting firms. See if they know anything."

"Let me know if you need anything." Kyle paused. "I'll text Dave." I heard a girl's voice in the background.

Trigger had done his business and was now flirting with a pug. "Sounds good. Later."

"Bye."

I took Trigger back into the apartment, hoping maybe Annie would meet me at the door naked.

But she was sitting on my bedspread, wearing a silky blue nightie, and texting on her phone.

I unleashed Trigger. "Anything important?"

"Oh, no. I mean, it's nothing. Chris just asked where I was because he'd stopped by my parents' house and they'd said I'd left."

"He just stops by your house whenever he feels like it?" I clenched my teeth. "Are you fucking kidding me, Annie? Are you still seeing him?"

"No, Pat. Of course not. But we're still friends. He went through a lot you know, being a suspect, everyone treating him like a murderer. And, I mean, he cares about me."

"Sure, he does. And he'll comfort you when I deploy, too. Have you slept with him since you've been home?"

"Oh, my God. No! Pat, you're crazy. We grew up together, our families know each other. He was so distraught when I went missing. It was hard on him, too."

My head heated up. "I bet. Don't play me, Annie. This can end now if you're going to fuck around on me. I don't need this bullshit, your dad bribing me, worrying about you when I'm in the field—"

"Bribe you? He tried to give you the reward. Which you should take. You deserve it. You can buy a condo with it."

Figures, I knew my lifestyle would never be enough to satisfy this fucking princess. "I'm sure Chris has a great condo. Maybe even a beachfront house. Go live with him if you don't like my crappy apartment."

The strap from her nightie fell off her shoulder and I could see her breasts. Great distraction technique.

"Pat, relax. That's not what I meant." She wrapped her naked legs around me. "I know your ex cheated on you. I'm not her. I would never do that to you. But I'm not sorry I texted Chris. He has a girlfriend. There is nothing going on between us. Nothing. I'm only interested in you. I swear."

This was a mistake. Going to her house, kissing her, inviting her back to my place. Even under the best of circumstances, it was hard to have a successful relationship with a Team guy. We had so much working against us. Her family, her past, my job, the way we met. And I hated to admit it, but it was hard for me to deal with the fact she had been a prostitute. I didn't blame her for it, nor think less of her. Nothing like that. I understood she had been forced. But at night, the images of all of those other men, random faceless men fucking her, filled my head, like a never-ending movie loop.

I unwrapped her legs. "I don't know if I can do this. We're too different."

"Get over yourself and think of me for a second."

"I am—"

"No, you're thinking of how I fit into your life. Think of me. What I want. What I need."

"I'm tired. I'm going to take a shower and then crash."

She nodded and I went into the bathroom and turned on the hot water. SEALs hated cold showers, reminded us of freezing our balls off in the ocean during BUD/S.

I was trying to push her away. I knew that. I couldn't risk letting her in and having her betray me also. But hadn't I already let her in?

I dried off and went back into the bedroom. Annie was lying under the covers, reading a book she must've grabbed from my nightstand. I needed to give her—us—a chance.

"Sorry. I trust you. I just don't trust him, or any guy for that matter. If he's your friend, I need to meet him."

Her voice became quiet. "Why?"

"Because I need to look him in the eyes. It's important to me."

"Fine. I'll ask him."

"Tomorrow. Lunch at two."

Her fingers moved across her phone. She smiled when she received a reply. Pissed me off. I wanted to be the only one to make her smile.

"He says okay."

Yeah, I'll bet. Fucking 'Jody', just like we sing about in our cadences—*"Your baby was lonely, as lonely could be, Til Jody provided the company."* He'll be happy to shake my hand tomorrow and fuck my girl when I'm gone.

I wanted to believe her words, the promises she made with her kisses. But now I wasn't sure. My next deployment wouldn't be easy. It's brutal going months without any communication. And if we were deep undercover, that's exactly what would happen. I'm sure Chris would be waiting with open arms to take care of her.

30. Annie

I WOKE, HOT, BREATHLESS, SCARED. For a second, I forgot where I was. But seeing Patrick splayed in the bed next to me quickly made me feel safe again.

I snuck out of bed, and crept into the living room. Gabriel was asleep on the pullout sofa, Trigger stood guard. Trigger's ears perked up when he saw me. As if to ask if I needed him for anything. I pet him on the head; he circled and lay back down.

The small kitchen was clearly the home of a bachelor—minimal appliances, refrigerator stocked with nothing more than beer, condiments, eggs, and bacon. My mind raced—I wanted to take care of Pat. Cook for him, love him, brighten up his life. Were we moving too fast? I knew it seemed antifeminist to say this, but all I wanted was Pat. I didn't care about my parents, my old friends, going back to school. For now. I couldn't help myself; I was falling in love with him. I wanted to be his wife, have him adopt Gabriel, create a family. Was that so wrong? God, how pathetic was I? He hadn't told me he loved me. He wouldn't even make love to me. Was this connection in my head? I had to know.

I poured myself a glass of water. Little things, like the freedom to get up in the middle of the night and leave my room, make a snack, get a drink, were still so enjoyable to me. I never took anything for granted.

But I was not healed. No matter how hard I wanted to be. Noises rattled me, I had to keep the window shades open at all times. Somehow, being with Pat again allowed my mind to calm down. Like I felt with him by my side, I'd never be in danger again. I was making progress in my journey back to myself.

I crept back into the bedroom. Pat was just collapsed on the bed, his strong back shined in the moonlight. He was so fucking fine, I couldn't believe it. I still felt guilt for being attracted to him, not sure why. Like because I was a prostitute, I shouldn't have sexual thoughts? I wanted him, completely. I imagined him making love to me, kissing me gently, tasting my flesh, licking me like an ice cream cone, making me come, begging me to scream his name. I needed him so fucking bad. But not just soft and loving. I wanted him to fuck me hard, his huge cock filling me up, making my pussy throb. Could Pat ever fuck me? Not make love to me but screw me senseless? Or would he always be worried about traumatizing me.

Either way, I couldn't handle the guilt. This insane sadness that I couldn't shake. I don't deserve love, I don't deserve sex, I don't deserve him. My father's voice rang in my head, telling me that Pat was worthless, a player. Real men don't buy girls, he said.

But I forgave Pat. Forgave him for going to a brothel. Forgave him for his words that echoed in my head, "Fine, we don't have to talk. Blow me." He didn't even see me back then. I was an object.

Pat was a good man. Not just because he saved me. That was his job, I got it. But the way he looked at me, the way he played with my child, the way he respectfully held himself back when I knew he wanted me. I could see his desire, every time he touched me. His level of self-control was unreal.

I cuddled up next to him, kissed his shoulders, his neck.

He turned to me. "Hey. You okay?"

"Yes babe. Sorry to wake you. I need you."

His strong arms pinned me under him. He pressed his hips into mine. I could feel his big, beautiful cock pressing against my panties. I wanted him, I wanted this, I needed to feel every inch of him.

No words. He kissed my neck, nibbled my ears. One hand pinned my wrists above my head, while his other hand worked its way down my body.

I still felt so dirty—why would he want to make love to me? Did he truly see me as beautiful like he claimed? Instead of the worthless woman he had hired to blow him?

My back arched, I wiggled free and his hand quickly released the hold on my wrists. A guilty look washed over his face.

"I'm sorry, Annie, did I hurt you?"

"No no, that's not it. I want you." I tugged at his boxers, his happy trail taunting me. I wanted to see him, feel him inside of me. "Make love to me, Pat."

His lips curled, and I glanced at his boxers. I could see his desire for me. "No, Annie, tonight is for you. All for you. Lie down."

I did, hesitantly. He knelt beside me, his knees by my hip and his hands on either side of my body. I watched him intently. I was scared, yet excited. What if I could never enjoy myself again?

My body trembled, and it was a feeling so sweet it made my heart hurt.

He smiled down at me as he lifted a hand to move the hair off my forehead. The stubble on his face tickled my skin. I shuddered, imagining him going further, that same stubble grazing my thighs. I closed my eyes at his soft touch, my back arching off the mattress with a loud creak. He trailed his hand down my face and along the line of my jaw. I sucked in a breath as his hand continued down my neck to follow the soft material of my nightie over the rise of my breast.

I opened my eyes. My fingers grasped at the sheets when he dipped a finger under my nightie to tease at my nipple. He moved his finger to pull the strap of my nightie, down my shoulder to bare my breasts. He trapped my arm under the strap and moved his head to take one into his mouth. My other hand pressed his head closer. He kept at one breast, and then lavished attention on the other until I was writhing under him.

"Pat, that feels amazing."

His tongue traveled from my chest, down the centerline to dip in my belly button. He nibbled down my stomach to the line of my panties. Nuzzling it with the scrape of his stubble caused me to gasp in pleasure.

"Babe, please. Don't stop." I wanted this, I wanted to feel pleasure. I wanted to see if my body could respond to his love.

His lips kissed my soft skin. I couldn't believe what he was about to do. I'd fantasized about this so many times, but I was afraid he would think I was dirty. His kisses erased that thought in my mind. He touched his tongue to my opening. My thighs clamped around his neck and my fingers grasped at his shoulders. My head arched back and I groaned with pleasure as his tongue fluttered over me.

I gasped for breath. I became wetter, hotter, hungrier for him. His pace varied, sweet loving to fast and frenzied. My body responded. I wasn't broken.

"Pat, don't stop, please, baby, you make me feel so good." My body bucked on the bed and, when he slipped two fingers deep inside me, I exploded around them with a moan for an endless moment and he eased up to watch the erotic response ripple across my face.

Complete bliss, which I never thought I would feel again.

I collapsed across the bed. A thousand spikes of pleasure still bounced through my body. I gasped in a final breath, savoring the moment. I had to tell him something.

"I love you."

I didn't expect a response. Maybe a cuddle, a kiss on the forehead, a loving touch.

The silent night echoed through the room. He wrapped his arms around me, pulled me to him.

I was drifting off to sleep, content with his embrace.

A few more seconds passed, and his words roused me from my haze. His lips parted. "I love you, too."

31. Patrick

ANNIE AND GABRIEL SLEPT IN late, but I couldn't rest. After making her come last night, I was worked up, so I just watched her sleep. I wanted to fuck her so badly but I had to be patient. Normally, and I know it makes me a fucking douche to say this, but I wasn't the type to have a woman stay over at my apartment. I couldn't afford those kinds of connections due to the amount of time I was on assignment. I simply didn't want the complication. With Annie though, I didn't have any objections to waking up with her shit all over my house or having her in my bed.

I snuck out to the farmer's market, came back, and made her breakfast in bed. I wasn't much of a chef, more of a short order cook—scrambled eggs, bacon, toast.

I told her I had to do something quick at work

and that I'd be back in an hour or so. She and Gabriel decided to take Trigger to the park.

I cruised over to Kyle's place. The lucky bastard had invested some of his NFL money in a sick townhouse overlooking the beach.

I rang the doorbell and a blonde girl opened the door wearing nothing but one of Kyle's jerseys and purple panties.

The girl didn't say anything, just turned and walked into the kitchen. I followed, and couldn't help staring at her fine ass. Had I never met Annie, I'd probably be hooking up with a different girl every night since I'd been home. Kyle and I would be living it up, maybe even hit the Playboy mansion. We always were invited courtesy of a Hollywood director who loved us. We'd trained his actors for one of the many action movies about the Bin Laden raid.

Kyle was sitting at his breakfast bar, reading the paper. He wore only pajama bottoms.

The girl went into the kitchen. "Want some breakfast?" She cracked an egg into a bowl.

"I'm good, thanks."

"My bad. Pat, this is Sara. Let her cook you breakfast."

"Sure." Every girl Kyle hooked up with tried to audition to be his wife. He wasn't like me—he believed in love and wanted to get married. But he still hadn't found what he was looking for.

Sara smiled, put some butter in the skillet. "So are you a former football player, too?"

I glared at Kyle, not knowing if he had even told this chick he was a SEAL. I doubted it. Kyle usually told people he was retired from the NFL.

"Nah, honey. Pat here's my personal trainer. Actually, we need to discuss my plans for the upcoming season in my office. Can you bring us our omelets when you're done?"

"Sure, babe."

Kyle stood up and kissed her, his right hand cupping her ass. I followed him into his office.

"Upcoming season? She thinks you still play ball?"

"I told her I used to play ball, might try out again."

"Really? That's news to me. You're kind of locked into a military contract."

"True that. But who knows, I could write a book about one of our missions and get kicked out."

I laughed. Five years ago, most SEALs wanted to remain anonymous. After the Bin Laden raid, every SEAL had a book deal, wanted to become an actor, or ran a Cross Fit. It was fucking ridiculous.

"When'd you meet her?"

"Last night. At PB Bar & Grill. She's a preschool teacher. I dig her. She could be the one."

"That's what you say every time."

Sara entered the room, carrying a tray with our food and two coffees. I thanked her. It was nice being taken care of for a change.

"Could you close the door?"

"Yup. Don't be too long." She licked her lips. "I'll be upstairs, waiting. Nice to meet you, Pat."

"You, too."

The door shut. I took a bite of my omelet—cheese and ham. Simple, but good.

"So how's Annie?"

"Good. She's back at my place now."

Kyle's mouth widened into a smile. "I knew it."

"Yeah, well, I caught her texting Chris. She says she's not screwing him but who knows?"

"Man, that Marissa chick screwed you up. Women can have male friends and not fuck them. It is possible. Just give Annie a chance. She's crazy about you, dude. And she's a good girl. Fine, strong, sweet. Not many women could survive what she did."

Kyle always seemed to be right. But I didn't come here to discuss my relationship problems. "Have you heard back from Dave?"

"Yup. He's waiting for our call. Going to conference him now."

Kyle dialed his number, and Dave's face popped up on Kyle's computer screen. You have to love modern technology.

"Hi, guys. So I've done some searching. Everyone in Aruba knew Annie was taken, but I guess they had her hidden out in Curaçao."

I nodded. "Yup. That's what she told me."

"As I told you on the ship, I'd heard of sightings of her, but nothing panned out. And, of course, all the locals know I'm a former SEAL so I'd be the last one they'd tell."

"Understood," Kyle said.

"Well about two years after she went missing, some contractors came around the island and asked about Annie. Flashing her picture everywhere. Rented my yacht."

"We know this—the fake SEAL. He had people with him?"

"No, Pat. Not him. That con man never even looked for her. I have my doubts he even exists."

I was confused. "I'm not following you."

"I told you on the boat, these men who came looking for her were former Team guys. They were very thorough and professional. They must've hit every brothel here and in Aruba. Yet there has never been any mention of them by Annie's family or the FBI."

My mind raced. "So, you think these guys were paid by her family but didn't find her?"

Dave's head shook. "No. I think they found her—and left her there."

What the fuck was he saying? "That makes no fucking sense."

"Hear me out. You found her by accident. These men worked for someone. Not the government. Annie had vanished. There were never any ransom notes, no one saw her get taken, her boyfriend was suspected of killing her or it was a possible suicide. Someone hired these guys, whoever they were, to find Annie. I did some more digging once I returned and one of my buddies swears that one of these guys was drunk and bragging that he had found her. And that other girl, Nicole. I bet they found them. They just decided not to bring them home."

Jesus! It made sense. There was no way with all the money her parents had that they hadn't found legit security contractors to locate her. Which group did they hire? And if they found her, why the hell didn't they bring her home?

Kyle took over the conversation. "What did the guys look like?"

"They looked like recently retired SEALs. Older, mid to late thirties. Clean cut, no tattoos, built. One of them was a ginger. I hope this helps."

"Thanks, Dave, I really appreciate it. Next time we're in town, I'll buy you a beer."

"Any time. Let me know if you need anything."

I stared at the empty screen, my mind totally blown.

Finally, Kyle broke my trance, "Has Annie mentioned any other Americans she, um, 'met' over there?"

"Nope. She doesn't talk about it."

"Well, I'll call Vic and we can start researching

older Team guys—see who's in contracting, any redheads. But you need to talk to your girlfriend, make sure we're on to something."

"I doubt she'll talk, but I'll try. Thanks, man."

"Any time. I need to take care of some business upstairs and then I'll get right on it."

I gave him a high five. "I get it. I'll let myself out."

I walked out of the house, but instead of getting back into my truck, I headed to the ocean. I needed to clear my head.

My gut clenched. I had to interrogate Annie about her johns without her getting suspicious.

In the worst of conditions, the legacy of my teammates steadies my resolve and silently guides my every deed. I will not fail.

32. Patrick

I RETURNED BACK TO MY apartment, carrying two iced mochas and chocolate milk from Bird Rock Coffee.

Annie greeted me with a kiss—and a clean apartment. She'd scrubbed my floors, dusted the furniture, and even folded my laundry. Fuck, I didn't remember getting married.

"Sorry, I hope you don't mind. I need to be busy."

I got it. And here I was about to interrogate her about her past.

"Gabriel's taking a nap."

We sat at the table.

"What's wrong, Pat? You're acting weird. Are you still upset about Chris? We're meeting him in an hour so—"

"No. That's not it."

"No secrets. Spill it."

I didn't know how to approach her. We had an unspoken rule never to talk about her time in the Caribbean. "In the brothel, when I came back to see if you were who you said you were, you told me that you and Nicole were convinced you were going to be saved. Why did you think that?"

She shifted in her seat. "Why do you ask?"

"Just curious."

"Why now?" She sucked her cheeks in.

"I've always wanted to ask you. There's never a right time."

"It was nothing. I thought this other guy was sent to save me once. He never came back. Why does it matter?"

"It matters to me. Why did you think he was going to come back?"

"First, you get all jealous about Chris and now you're interrogating me about the johns? You know I don't want to talk about them."

"Please, Annie. I have to know."

Her hands clenched into fists. "What do you want me to say? You want to hear how he forced me to make out with Nicole? What positions he fucked me in? Will that make you happy?"

"Dammit, Annie. Is that what you think of me? Of course, I don't want to know that shit. You don't think it kills me that all those men used you? That I used you? Every fucking night since I met you, I have nightmares of faceless men who fuck you. And in them, I'm fucking helpless and can't save you. I want to kill every man who has ever touched you. I just wanted to fucking try to understand why no one ever saved you. Is that so fucking wrong?"

She pulled out her hair, like she had on the night I'd returned to the brothel. "I'm sorry, Pat. I'm just so screwed up. I lost it. I hate myself."

"I'm not mad at you." I pulled her to me, and kissed her forehead. "I know this is hard for you. I've been thinking about it and I want to know. But if you don't want to tell me that's fine." I wasn't using reverse psychology—I didn't want to upset her further. She'd tell me when she was ready.

"I'm sorry," she squeaked.

"I'm sorry I brought it up. Forget I asked. We need to leave soon to meet your boyfriend."

"Ha ha. I'll get ready."

Annie emerged from the bathroom wearing a short skirt, a tank top, and strappy sandals. Granted it was eighty degrees, but she looked too damn hot to go outside.

"What are you wearing?"

"Jesus, Pat. Controlling much? It's scorching out and I thought you'd like it. I bought it yesterday. Now you're going to tell me what to wear? I was a hooker, I'm beyond modesty."

My throat became dry. We weren't communicating at all. "No, I'm not telling you what to wear. But we're going to meet your ex-boyfriend. I already don't trust him, and I don't need him lusting after you in front of me. You can wear whatever you want. It's going to be so fucking hard for me to be away from you when I deploy next month and you're not making it any easier."

"So, if I dress sexy it will be harder for you to trust me? That's dumb." She wasn't backing down.

"That's not what I'm saying. I trust you. He's your ex. I'm a man—I know what he's going to think when he sees you. You're fucking hot."

She shrugged. "Okay. I'll change."

God, was I that much of a paranoid asshole? I wasn't one of those men who thought women who dressed sexy were asking for it. I just wanted to protect Annie. I didn't want anyone fantasizing about her. It would be impossible for me to focus on my job if I were worried sick about every man eye-fucking my woman while I was away.

She came back out in longer shorts, a tee shirt, and the same strappy sandals.

I kissed her. "You still look hot. Thank you."

"It's not a big deal. I get it." She rested her head on my chest. "Thanks."

"For what?"

"For being honest with me about your feelings. I want you to be able to trust me. I didn't realize how hard it would be for you to accept my past. I knew you wouldn't judge me for what happened, but I forget that it must be tough for you to think about me being with those guys. What I'm saying is, it means a lot to me that you want to be with me."

"I'm not going to lie to you and say this is easy for me. Because it isn't. No man wants to picture anyone touching his girl ever, let alone hundreds. I know it wasn't your choice. I know it wasn't your fault. In my head, that girl was Star."

She had a gleam in her eye, like an inner glow from her soul. "But for me, I feel like you're the only man who gets me. Because you saw me as Star. And you're still here. You haven't only read about my past, you saw me first-hand like that. Fuck, I mean, you hired me. Star is a part of me and I don't want to forget about her. Ever. If it weren't for Star, there would be no Gabriel. She made me strong. Nothing can shake me now. I've made peace with my past, getting taken, the rapes, the drugs, and the men. Yeah, it was a nightmare. But it was my path. I was meant to be Gabriel's mother. I was meant to find you. Therapy and yoga help me to understand that. I forgive my kidnappers. I feel like I can do anything, endure anything."

I was mesmerized by her. Her forgiveness for the men who took her blew my mind. I never forgave people, my ex, the guy who hurt my mom. Annie was a better person than I was. She made me want to become a better person.

We woke Gabriel up, got him ready, leashed up Trigger, and we walked out the door.

Annie constantly amazed me with how strong

she was. In BUD/S, the men who made it through weren't necessarily the strongest men, the fastest men, or the smartest men. But they were the ones who, on day one, were determined not to quit, no matter what. They would not ring that bell.

Annie was like the men who made it. No matter how hard her life had been, she had been determined not to ring that bell under any circumstances. She was exactly like me. She could survive anything.

Maybe even loving me.

We drove to Solana Beach to meet Chris. He had picked the place, Zinc Café. I didn't care; I just wanted to look him in his eyes and hear him say there was nothing going on between them.

The place was dog friendly, so Trigger made himself right at home. We walked into the courtyard, and spotted Chris sitting at a table, drinking iced tea.

He hugged Annie, and gave Gabriel a high five. I made sure to study his body language with Annie. He wanted her for sure. Fuck.

"Nice to meet you. Thank you for saving her."

He shook my hand—a decent handshake. He looked older than the pictures I'd seen of him on the web. His sun-streaked hair was long and brushed his shoulders, his tan skin was weathered, and his eyes had lines around them.

"I'm going to order for us." Annie kissed me on

the cheek and squeezed my hand. I knew she was telling me to be nice to him. She didn't have a clue that I had an additional ulterior motive for wanting to meet him.

Annie and Gabriel left us and went to order at the counter.

Chris smiled at me. "I wanted to thank you for clearing my name. I know finding Annie was way more important and it's not about me, but it's hard walking around having everyone look at you like a murderer. I felt so fucking guilty because I didn't know what happened to her. I was depressed thinking she died, or was out there being traded around. I mean, I should've been able to protect her, but I didn't. We were only eighteen and so stupid. I want to tell you that there is nothing going on between us, either. I'm seeing someone."

I'm glad he got that out of the way, though I was pretty sure Annie had texted him to tell me that. He made strong eye contact and I believed him, even though I could tell he was still attracted to her. Not that I could blame him. "Thanks for that. I trust her. That's not why I wanted to meet you, man." I glanced over at Annie. She was talking to the cashier. "What do you know about her dad?"

Trigger sniffed Chris. "Mr. Hamilton? He's great. Our fathers are old golfing buddies. He always believed I had nothing to do with Annie's disappearance. Why?"

I wasn't going to answer his questions. "How's

his relationship with Annie?"

A gust of wind blew his hair into his face. "He's a tough guy, that's for sure. Very hard on Annie. Total perfectionist. When we were dating, he was always giving her a hard time about everything. Her grades, her clothes, her friends. And we hadn't even told our parents when we went on the vacation. He's old-fashioned and Annie was sure he'd forbid her to go. I think, in all honesty, he's embarrassed more than anything. He can't handle the fact she was a hooker. And I think seeing Gabriel, knowing his father kidnapped Annie, is painful for him."

Made complete sense. Her dad cared more about his image than his own daughter. He couldn't handle the shame he felt she brought on the family, so he left her to die. "It's hard for me to deal with, too. But it wasn't her fault."

He leaned into me. "Man, I got to hand it to you. You're the man. I respect the fuck out of what you do, being a SEAL. You saved her. But how do you deal with the fact that she's been with so many men? I know it wasn't her fault. But you're a better man than me. It would drive me crazy."

"I try not to think about it." I hated to admit it, but I liked Chris. He was honest and respectful.

Annie returned carrying three plates, like a waitress. She placed a burger in front of me, and Gabriel climbed into my lap.

I took a bite. It tasted great, but there was one

problem. "Did you order me a veggie burger?"

"That's the only kind of burger they have. This place is vegetarian."

Figured. I was not cut out for the surfer lifestyle.

"So, are you guys best friends yet?" Annie teased.

Chris dug his fork into some kind of weird grainy salad. Quinoa? Bulgur? No clue. "You bet. Hey, do you think you could ever give me a tour of the base? I'd love to see the obstacle course."

"Sure, buddy." This guy was more of a fan than a threat. I was glad I met him.

"See? I knew you two would hit it off."

The rest of the lunch was uneventful. Chris talked about some surf competition he'd entered; I guess the guy was pretty good. Seeing them together gave me a small glimpse of who Annie had been before she'd been taken: carefree, laid back, and sweet. She had probably been the type of girl who would've never even considered dating a SEAL.

Annie went back into the café to get some boxes.

Chris stood up. "Nice meeting you, Pat. If you ever need anything, let me know. And I'll always be here for Annie, even when you're gone. But you don't have to worry about us hooking up. I'd never do that to you. Seriously, dude. You finding her was the best thing that ever happened to me. You not only gave Annie her life back, you gave me back mine."

"I'll have a beer with you anytime, Chris. And let me know when you want to see the base."

"I will. That would be awesome. Hit me up if you ever want to ride the waves with me."

I had no desire to learn. I'd never surfed, and I spent enough time in the water. But, I'd try anything once. "Sounds good. Later, bro."

Annie walked back out of the café, carrying a paper bag. "Bye, Chris."

They hugged again and I stared at Trigger. Friends. That's all they were.

We climbed into my truck and Annie had a big grin on her face.

"What?"

"I knew you'd like him."

"He's cool. Different than how I thought he'd be."

"See?" She rubbed my thigh. "I told you nothing was going on."

We backed out of the parking lot, and drove away. She squeezed my hand.

Later that night, after Gabriel went to sleep, Annie cuddled up to me. "I'll tell you what happened."

"It's okay. You don't have to."

"No. I want to. I'm calm now. I just have to separate the experience from myself, you know? I have to be in the right state of mind to talk about it."

I nodded. Looking in her eyes would make this conversation too painful. For her. For me.

She took a deep breath and spoke in a whisper. "About two years after I was taken, these two American men came to the brothel. Not the same one you met me at, but a different one in Aruba. They were in their mid-thirties, one guy had brown hair and one guy was a redhead."

Holy shit. My muscles quivered. Dave was right. I didn't want Annie to see any reaction from me. "Go on."

"Well, the first time they showed up, they chose two other girls. But I swear to God they both recognized me. When you picked me, you barely gave me a second glance, but the pimp allowed customers to 'check out the merchandise'. The redhead got right in my face, as he walked down the line. Looked straight at me, even stared at my ankle, like he was looking for my tattoo, you know? I thought for sure he was going to pick me that night, but he didn't. Around a week later they returned, but this time they chose Nicole and me. We'd been picked together before, sickos wanting to watch some girl on girl action. We were both cautious yet hopeful, thinking maybe they would recognize us. I mean, they were American."

I ground my teeth. This was almost unreal.

"We went back to the room. They didn't talk, just kind of motioned at us what they wanted us to do. To each other. Then to both of them." Her hands made fists. I wanted to take my gun out and shoot something. "So after that, they just kind of laid there. They didn't bolt like most guys do." She pointed at me.

Guilty.

"So, I thought they recognized us. I was so excited and still had hope back then. I opened my mouth to tell them our names, but Nicole stopped me. She didn't want to get in trouble. I didn't care. Nicole had this look of sheer terror. The redhead, I remember, took this long, like, pained breath. I thought for sure he knew our stories, who we were. But the other man, he was really cold. He stood up and they left. The redhead looked back at me when he left the room and mouthed, 'I'm sorry.' I knew he recognized me. I was so positive he was going to come back. And I guess I'd even convinced Nicole we were going to be rescued. That at least they would share the sighting with my folks, and someone would come save us."

My ears pounded. These motherfuckers, possibly former SEALs, found these two Americans there, and left them to die! They couldn't be SEALs; we were bound to a higher code.

Uncompromising integrity is my standard. My character and honor are steadfast.

Granted, I clearly didn't always live my life with uncompromising integrity. But I couldn't fathom these men leaving these girls, knowing they were trafficked.

Her hand was shaking now. "But after six

months, nothing. I was so fucking mad at them. I mean, why couldn't they tell someone? This was my life that had been stolen. I was a sex slave. How could they recognize us and do nothing? And I was pissed at myself for believing I would be saved. Nicole lost it. I mean, she went crazy. Started mouthing off to the pimps, refusing clients, even begging for extra heroin. I pleaded with her to stay strong. We would find a way out. Somehow. Someday. Together. But she wanted to die. She stole my drugs, and some from a few other girls and shot herself up. And I wanted to die, too. But I had Gabriel. I had to hope for him. I couldn't stop feeling sorry for myself. Why me? Of all the girls who got drunk on spring break, why me? Then I remembered years ago hearing about a girl who had been kidnapped for ten years and escaped. It was possible. So why should I give up? I had to get out—for me, for Gabriel, for Nicole. I had a life to live. I had to survive no matter what. That's when I made the decision not to give up. The next time I met a man who I even thought could save me, I would take the chance. Risk it all."

I held her, stroked her forehead. "Thanks for telling me. It means a lot to me. I'm not going to leave you, Annie. I'll always be here for you."

"You're my hero."

We didn't talk for the remainder of the night. Yet, my thoughts raced. There was no more doubt. I was one hundred percent committed to Annie.

Committed to making her happy.

But I still didn't have the entire story straight. Who were these men, who hired them, and why did they leave the two girls behind, when they were completely capable of saving them?

The only thing I was sure of was I wouldn't rest until I found out what the fuck was going on.

33. Annie

WHY DID PAT WANT TO know? What was he up to?

No one knew what happened in the brothel. I hadn't uttered a word, besides that basic timeline and facts to anyone. Not my parents, not my therapist. Not even Pat. My father had convinced me that sharing my sob story would turn me into a media target, endanger my life and the life of my child. Reporters, photographers would stalk me. People in the grocery store would look at me with a combination of disgust and pity. Gabriel would be ostracized at school—teased for what his father had done to me.

But was my father right?

I felt free, liberated. Telling Pat gave me a sense of strength. Healing.

I couldn't keep these secrets bottled up inside

me. I had to tell my story. Maybe it would help people. Women, make them more cautious on vacation. Or if an innocent girl heard my story today, maybe one day if she had the misfortune of ever being kidnapped, she would remember hearing my story. My words, my rescue, my hope. I remember hearing about other women captives that had been freed. Their stories kept me going when I'd lost my way. If my story could do that for one woman, it would be worth it.

But I couldn't. My mouth was bound, I was gagged. Just how I had been in the brothel. But not by my captor. No. By my father. I didn't want to disgrace him further. It was bad enough that people thought I'd run away, and that fake story had quickly died down in the media. The truth, though, would make me a household name. And my infamy would never go away.

But it wasn't about me. I had to think about Gabriel. My parents. And even Pat. Yes, oh God. Pat. I couldn't let his story get out. It would ruin his career. Hiring me at the brothel, going rogue to save me. His face and name would be splashed all over the tabloids. And it would ruin any chance of us finding happiness together. Nothing was worth that risk.

I loved him, he said he loved me. And he loved my son.

One day, I would tell my truth. Maybe years

from now, when Gabriel was grown, when my parents had passed, when Pat had retired. But for now, my story will remain buried deep inside my head, my heart, my soul.

34. Patrick

I TOLD ANNIE I HAD to work the next day. I headed back to Kyle's house, but this time, instead of Sara opening the door, I was greeted by Vic.

"Hey, man, come inside. I think we've got something."

I followed Vic back to Kyle's office. Kyle was in Intel and made mission plans like they were football plays—there were pictures, diagrams, timelines, and maps. Luckily, his security clearance gave him access to SEAL service records.

I sat on one of the chairs. "What do we have?"

Kyle looked up at me. "Well, I made a list of all men who left the Teams in the last five years. Then I eliminated all the men who went into non-security-related careers. I was left with one hundred and forty-three names. They were spread out among different countries, different states, and different contractors. There were only three gingers. Two of them still work at their security companies, but one of them worked for Neptune Group. He left his security detail around three years ago."

"Six months after he found Annie."

"Exactly. Name is Matt Houston. I asked some buddies who knew him, looks like he checked into drug rehab. And get this, he lives in Poway."

Vic jumped in. "And we're meeting him for lunch in an hour. I fed him some bullshit that I'm thinking about contributing to a foundation for fallen SEALs. He ate it up. Was happy to meet with some Team guys."

Brilliant. Team guys always welcomed meetings from fellow Frogs, even if they had never met before. That was one of the benefits of being part of the best fraternity in the world.

We headed inland in Kyle's Black Cadillac Escalade Hybrid. I texted Annie to see how she was doing. I wanted to spend as much time as possible with her before I had to deploy, but I needed to find out the truth.

Matt had recommended we meet at Brothers Provisions, a sandwich shop which served craft beer on tap in Rancho Bernardo, a town next to Poway.

As we approached, I scanned the patio. I recognized him immediately. Red hair, still built, looked hardened. I didn't care if he was a Team guy—I wanted to kill this motherfucker for fucking my girl and leaving her to die.

"Hey, Matt. I'm Pat, this is Kyle and this is Vic." I reached out my hand, but he didn't take it. His hands had an unsteady twitch, and he was rattling his keys.

He nodded his head, and we all went inside to order sandwiches and beers. Back out on the patio, we made small talk—Teams we'd been on, guys we both knew, and deployments.

He took a sip of his beer, and his eyes shifted back and forth. "I need to hit the head."

He stood up and went inside the shop. Barely a few seconds had passed when an older-model black Ford truck barreled out of the parking lot. He'd been on to us.

We didn't speak; we knew what to do. I threw down some money for a tip and we hightailed it into Kyle's Escalade.

I could see Matt's truck entering I-15 Freeway going south.

Kyle chased him down the freeway, dodging in and out of cars. Matt didn't slow down. Where the fuck was he going?

I didn't have time for this shit. He slowed to enter the 56 West and I took out my pistol, leaned out the window and shot out his back right tire.

He pulled to the shoulder of the freeway, Kyle's Escalade right behind him.

I saw him reach toward his glove compartment.

This motherfucker was going to kill himself. Or us.

We jumped out of the car, our weapons ready.

I approached the vehicle. He had the gun aimed right at me. "You have about ten seconds to unfuck yourself, Matt. Put down the gun. We're not here to kill you. Don't do anything stupid."

He kept the gun steady. "He sent you. I didn't talk to anyone."

"No one sent us. We're the ones who saved Annie. We did some digging. We just want to talk to you."

With three guns pointed at his head, he didn't have much choice. Kyle disarmed Matt without a struggle. I slid into the passenger seat of his truck and handed Matt's keys to Kyle. I told Vic to get Matt's spare tire out just in case a cop drove by and thought we looked suspicious. Kyle stood guard on the side of Matt's truck.

I needed some answers. "Start talking, asshole. Why did you leave her there?"

He blinked. The creases around his burdened eyes were so deep they looked as if they had been beveled with a blade. "First off, it's not my fault, man. I tried to save her. You have to know that. It started out like a standard job. Missing girl, possibly trafficked. Go to the island and see if she's alive, if you can find her."

"Who hired you?"

"Her father. Paid three hundred thousand dollars. Taylor, another former Team guy, and I volunteered. Seemed like a piece of cake—go hang out on Aruba for a month, all expenses paid, drink, snorkel, rescue a girl, and come home. We went down there, started fishing around. Asking locals. Visiting brothels. We had a tip a girl who matched Annie's description was at this one brothel. We cased the place. The first time we went in, our only goal was to see if we thought it was her, identify the tattoo and see what kind of shape she was in. The minute I saw her, I was positive it was Annie. Her hazel eyes, hair, tattoo, scar, and height. But we were ordered by our bosses to pick other girls that first night and not her."

His eyes focused ahead on some red lights from a construction truck. I tapped him over the head to get him to keep talking.

"I was so fucking stoked that day . . . to think I'd found this kidnapped girl and we'd be bringing her home in a week or so. The girl she was with, Nicole, we didn't even know she was there. That was a stroke of luck finding her. Of course, we'd read about her disappearance in Aruba, and we knew about her. I thought I'd be a fucking hero—saving two Americans. Collect her reward, too."

Cars whizzed by on the freeway. I looked in the rear view mirror, and Vic had the car jack out. "So what the fuck happened? Why did you leave her there?"

"I didn't have a fucking choice. We did some

more searching, about the brothel, the pimp, and the dancer who took her. Surveillance on Annie. At night, after all the clients left, she had a baby with her. Cute little boy, around six months old or so. We checked in with our bosses, after we found her in the brothel and they reported back to her father about Annie and the baby. We had a conference call with the motherfucker. He asked me how certain I was it was her, if she looked high, her demeanor, what she was wearing. I told him I'd bet my Trident it was his daughter. She was definitely a heroin user. I saw tracks on her arms when the pimp let me check her out. Then he asked me about the baby. If I was certain he was her son. I told him I couldn't be one hundred percent, but she saw him every night and I thought he was hers."

He turned to me, his eyes almost tearful. "As long as I live, I will never forget the next words out of his mouth. 'Leave her there. Forget you ever saw her. With any luck, she'll overdose soon.'"

My pulse quickened, and I wanted to shoot this motherfucker and save a bullet for Annie's dad. Gabriel was in danger. I was a professional warrior; I knew how to control my emotions. But this was unbelievable. What if her father had a plot to get rid of him, destroy any proof of Annie's past? I had to get Annie and Gabriel away from her family.

"Believe me, man. I begged him to reconsider. I told him we could detox her, and she'd be hailed as a survivor. And with therapy she could integrate back into society. He wouldn't consider it. He firmly reminded me of the one million dollar non-disclosure agreement I'd signed. I didn't have a fucking choice. I haven't ever told anyone, until today. You can't tell anyone—we have an unbreakable code."

"I won't." He was right. We would never repeat what he was telling us to anyone. Especially since he knew we'd been the ones to rescue Annie. He could ruin our careers. If I hadn't told him, he would've never talked to me. I needed to know the truth about Annie's dad.

"I racked my brain, thinking of anything I could do to save her. Go rogue; convince my partner to back me. But he wouldn't even discuss it, and I couldn't do it myself. We were ordered to go back a final time to verify with one hundred percent certainty that it was Annie. Which we did."

He paused and I wondered if he was reminiscing about fucking Annie, remembering her and Nicole going to town on each other. His own personal porno. I watched Matt's thin lips and I pictured them all over Annie's body. Her stroking his limp dick. My hand was on the trigger of my gun.

Give me an excuse to kill you motherfucker.

"Leaving them in that room was the hardest thing I'd ever done. Knowing I'd found them, but was abandoning them to die. I told the girls I was sorry, and walked out the door. When I returned to the States, I finished my remaining contracts and quit. I couldn't work with people with no integrity. Private contract work is nothing like being in the Teams. There's no morals, no law."

I sat there in silence. Completely blown away. I couldn't even process all the emotions I was feeling.

Finally, I broke the silence. "Nicole died. She overdosed six months later. She'd be alive today if you hadn't been such a pussy."

He squeezed his eyes shut. "I figured she did. I fucking hate myself, man. I drank myself into oblivion, started doing coke. Ended up in rehab. Don't have a girl, or a job, living off the disability I get from the VA. I mean, being on the Teams was my life. I was a great SEAL. I'm sure you guys know that, if you did your research on me. Nothing was more important to me than being the best warrior I could be. I pushed away my girlfriend, my family, and my friends. Always used the excuse she couldn't be faithful when I was away, or I would be a horrible husband because of my job. I stalked my ex on Facebook recently. She's a great woman, married to a Marine, and has two beautiful boys. I fucking loved her, but I completely fucked that relationship up. Cheated on her, lied to her. Thought everyone should kiss the ground I walked on and take my bullshit because I was a SEAL. I used to be just like you guys, and now I'm the old

Team guy in the bar, reliving my glory days when I play So Com in my apartment."

I'd had enough. I didn't want to listen to his sob story anymore. But every word he said resonated with me. "You could've saved her. Despite her dad. At least fucking told someone, *anyone*, she was alive. You condemned her to three more years of hell. And Nicole's death is on you. There is no excuse for that. '*I serve with honor on and off the battlefield.*' Remember our code?"

He squinted his eyes. "Don't fucking judge me. You're just like me. I didn't have a choice."

"No, Matt. I'm nothing like you. I met Annie in a brothel. Hired her. But unlike you, I came back. I saved her. I risked my job, my life, for her. That's what we do. That's our oath."

I voluntarily accept the inherent hazards of my profession, placing the welfare and security of others before my own.

I needed to get the fuck out of his truck. Imagining his hands all over my Annie made me want to pop him in the head. "I won't tell anyone. Not for your sake, but for Annie's. You better continue to keep your mouth shut."

We exited the vehicle, and Matt began to change his tire. Vic, Kyle and I bailed shortly after. I'd given my word to Matt that I wouldn't tell Annie I met him. And I never lied to SEALs, even former ones. I had to come up with another route. I needed to protect Annie and Gabriel from her father.

35. Patrick

I STOPPED AT THE FLORIST near my house. I chose for Annie a bouquet of wild flowers, nothing too pure and pretty. Carefree, damaged, and finally free, just like her. Matt had rattled me. I didn't want to end up like him. Annie was my perfect match: strong, loyal, and a survivor. I wanted her and Gabriel in my life forever. And her smoking body didn't hurt either.

Before I went home, I made one more pit stop. I had a surprise for Annie.

After my errands, I opened the door and Annie was sitting out on my small balcony, Trigger at her feet, Gabriel coloring. She wasn't reading, on her phone, or listening to music. Just staring outside. I admired her ability to enjoy each moment of freedom, without having to always be busy. I needed to learn to do that. Maybe she could teach me.

"Hey, babe."

Her face lit up when she saw me. She bounded over to me and gave me a kiss. "These are gorgeous. Thank you. How was work?"

I winced. I hated lying to her. I vowed to be honest with her from now on, but I couldn't tell her where I'd been. I didn't want to hurt her. "Good. An old Team guy stopped by." I turned to Gabriel. "Hey buddy, do you want to go to Disneyland? See the Monsters?"

"Monsters? I go see monsters?" Gabriel loved *Monsters University.*

"Let's get out of here." I had plenty of other suggestions, but they all seemed wrong. My first thought was a marine style park with killer whales but I doubted Annie wanted to spend the day watching animals kidnapped and forced into captivity to perform tricks for strangers.

"Disneyland? Yes. I'd love to."

I hadn't been to Disneyland since I was a kid. "Pack a bag. Let's go."

Her face brightened. I surprised myself by how much I enjoyed making her happy.

I sent Kyle a quick text.

An hour later, we were headed up the I-5 to Anaheim.

We pulled into the Downtown Disney parking lot and dropped Trigger off at the Disneyland Kennels just outside the gate. We headed straight over to Disney California Adventure Park, a first for me. Gabriel was having a blast. The first ride we hit was Monstropolis. He still didn't talk much, but watching him run around, smiling and carefree, filled me with pride. He was a sweet boy. How could his grandfather want nothing to do with him? We used our fast pass for Soarin' Over California, which I actually loved: seeing all the beautiful parks, lakes, and monuments of my home state made me happy to be back home. Normally when I was on leave, I was itching to return back to sea. For the first time in memory, I was finding joy in everyday life. Spending time with Annie and Gabriel made everything more enjoyable.

We hit some more rides, hopped over to Disneyland, and grabbed a quick bite to eat.

Annie was enjoying herself, but I knew this wasn't really her scene, even though she was trying her best for Gabriel. She hated crowds, and was pretty jumpy with the loud noises from the rides.

"I'm ready to go, Pat. But I need to do something first."

We walked to the main entrance of Disneyland, and Annie's eyes were glued to the ground. There were hundreds of tiny memorial pavers. She paced up and down the rows and finally stopped. There was a small one which read: The Race Family. December 8, 2006.

Annie knelt down and traced the stone with her hands. Tears filled her eyes. I didn't want to ruin her moment, so I stood back, unsure of what to say. She took out some Krazy Glue from her purse. She removed the necklace she'd worn in the brothel when I first met her, the rusty one with the key charm. She took the chain off, and glued it to Nicole's paver.

Shit, it even made me want to cry.

Annie took a picture of the paver and sat down.

After around ten minutes, Annie stood up. "We can go now."

"That was sweet, Annie."

"Yeah. I wanted her to have it. I'd be dead if it wasn't for her. She always talked about that vacation. How much fun they all had, and she was determined to come back here. One day, when I tell my story, I will go see her parents. Would you go with me to see them?"

"Of course."

"That would be great. Thank you."

This fake lie that Annie was living was preventing her from healing. She needed to tell the world what really happened. I put my arm around her, and pushed a tired Gabriel in the stroller. We picked up Trigger at the kennels, and headed back to the car.

"Where are we staying?"

"I have a surprise for you."

"I hate surprises. We're not staying near Disneyland?"

"Why don't you crash? It's a long drive. We'll be there by morning."

She tapped her fingers on the window. "Okay. This better be good." She leaned in and gave me a kiss.

I stopped by a drive-through Starbucks and ordered a venti black coffee, chocolate milk, and a few bottles of water for the drive.

Eight hours later, we had arrived at our destination just as the sun was coming up. Annie was still passed out in the seat next to me, Gabriel asleep in his car seat in the back.

"Wake up, sunshine. We're here."

She rubbed her eyes and blinked a few times to gain sight. The vast, pure lake glimmered in the sunrise.

"Pat! Tahoe! You remembered?"

"Of course. I never forget anything. Kyle has a buddy with a cabin in Incline Village. We have it for the whole week."

"The week? That's amazing." She leaned in to my seat and wrapped her arms around my neck, planting a kiss on my cheek.

I kissed her back. I couldn't wait to get her into the cabin. I scooped Gabriel out of his car seat, still asleep, and we took him into the cabin and into bed.

Annie was unlike any girl I'd ever known. She didn't expect anything of me, didn't try to change me, and accepted me for who I was. Maybe being with me the three months out of the year I didn't deploy would be enough to make her happy. I was crazy about her.

I had to confront her father, protect her and Gabriel from him. And I knew doing so would shatter Annie's carefully rebuilt world.

Kyle left out a detail about the owner of the cabin—apparently the guy was loaded. Probably one of his NFL buddies. The cabin was on the water in Incline Village, a hotspot of wealthy Silicon Valley executives. My mom and I used to stay in a crappy motel in South Lake Tahoe, but I loved it anyway. Annie and I checked the cabin out. The place had stonework, beautiful hardwood floors, seven bedrooms, a gourmet kitchen, a game room, an exercise room, a wine cellar, and a master bedroom with a private fireplace.

I needed to sleep. I let Trigger out back in the yard. "Can you bring him back in when he's done?"

She nodded.

I brought our bags in, then went upstairs to take a shower.

I took off my clothes and turned on the hot water. Should I confront her dad? It was pointless, really. He would either lie and deny it, or admit it and retaliate against Matt. No wonder her father hated my guts, probably knew I would figure his bullshit out, and was pissed I had saved Annie and Gabriel. Some may look at us enlisted SEALs as nothing more than brawn, but to get through BUD/S you had to be intelligent.

If I told Annie, she would have no one left in her life but me—and that was if she believed me. You never know, blood is thicker than water. And if I were all she had, who would be there for her when I was gone for months on end?

I stepped out of the shower and went into the bedroom. The fireplace was already on and Annie was sitting on the bed in some damn sexy lingerie. Pink silk nightie trimmed with black lace, split up high on her thigh. Damn.

I stopped in the doorway to watch as she smoothed lotion over her legs and it occurred to me I wouldn't mind seeing her do this every night. I'd heard the poor bastards in the Teams wax poetic about coming home to their wives and it wasn't until I saw her looking at home in the bed that I realized what they meant.

She looked up and saw me watching her. "Hey, Hero."

"You're hotter than that fire."

"So are you, standing there with nothing except a towel wrapped around your waist. Come here."

I walked over to the edge of the bed. She set the lotion on the nightstand, stood up, and took off my towel. She kissed my mouth, my chest, traced my scars, and worked her way down to my waist. I gently pushed her away from me.

We couldn't do this. Not yet.

"Pat, please. Come on, why are we waiting? I love you."

Those three words made me want her even more. But we'd waited this long, what was a few more days.

"Babe, I'm sorry. I love you, too. I need to sleep."

She slumped on the bed, pulling the cover over her body. "Are you not attracted to me? Is this because you still have a problem that I was a sex slave?"

Dammit. She didn't understand me at all. I didn't want her to feel rejected. I wanted her completely. Next time I was stuck in a dirt hole in the middle of Afghanistan, I wanted to dream of her. Or freezing my balls off in the frigid water in a swift boat, waiting to kill some pirates, I wanted the thought of coming home to her to keep me going. I wanted to make sure I was the only man to ever make her come, touch her, protect her, and take care of her.

"No, babe. Not at all. I want you so bad it hurts. I can't wait to make love to you. Just not tonight. Soon, I promise."

"Okay."

I wrapped my arms around her.

A sense of clarity washed over me. No more doubts. I wanted to make her mine, forever. She and Gabriel. They would never have to apologize or lie about who they were. I loved and accepted them completely.

Now there was only one question—would Annie say yes?

36. Patrick

EVEN THOUGH I LOVED TO ski and snowboard, I preferred summer to winter in Tahoe. The water was so blue and clear. We planned a hike on the Horsetail Falls Trail. It was a fairly easy hike which Gabriel could do, and not too crowded that our view would be spoiled.

We ambled along Pyramid Creek. I peeked through the trees until I found a great swimming hole. No one was around, so we changed into our swimsuits and dipped into our private pool. Gabriel was having a blast splashing around.

I climbed out, got dressed, and found a large, flat boulder for our picnic. I set all the food out, and poured three glasses of water. Annie and Gabriel were still wading in the swimming hole. She looked so blissful. I could stare at her forever.

I helped Gabriel out of the water and fed him

lunch. Annie finally emerged, looking like one of those water nymphs. She gathered her clothes and I checked out her perky ass.

The sky didn't have a cloud in sight, and the crisp air was almost like a drug to me. There were snow-capped mountains in the distance. After forever at sea, I couldn't imagine a more beautiful sight. After five years of captivity, I'm sure the view meant even more to Annie.

She took a sip of her water. "So, when you deploy next month, where are you going?"

"Middle East."

She nodded. "How will I communicate with you? Do you even have a phone?"

"Well, when we're on ship or one of the bases, I can check email. Maybe even use the phone. But if I'm out on an operation, it might be a month or so with no word."

Her lip trembled. I knew it would suck for her to get this close to me and then be left without a way to even contact me.

"Can I call someone? I mean, to see if you are okay?"

I took a bite of my sandwich. This was a talk we needed to have sooner or later. "Well, the wives have a number to call, and groups to meet at. But there isn't really something set up for girlfriends."

She shrugged her shoulders, then turned around to get more water out of the backpack. "I get it. I'll just call Vic's mom or Tori."

"Or you could just marry me."

"Ha. Ha."

When she turned back around, I had a surprise for her. I dropped to one knee.

"Pat, what are you doing?" her voice quaked.

"Will you marry me?" I held a small, princess cut diamond ring I'd purchased the other day.

"Are you serious?"

"I love you, Annie. And I love Gabriel. I want to adopt him. You're not damaged, you're the strongest woman I've ever met. You'd make a great Team wife. Plus, I've gone months on end without sex. I'm patient, I can wait for you. I'll help you heal. I don't want another man ever touching you again. You're mine. All mine. I'll be able to take care of you, always and forever. I'll do anything for you. Just say yes."

Her bottom lip quivered. She loved me, I knew that, but I also knew she didn't see this coming from a mile away. The thing she didn't understand was she was it for me. And the only way this would ever work out, with my job and her father, was if she became completely mine.

"You really love me?" she whispered.

Of course I did. "I love you, Annie. Completely."

She closed her eyes. I wished I could climb inside her head. Crush out her bad memories and replace them with good ones. But I couldn't do that. The only thing I could do was take care of her for the rest of her life and make sure no one ever harmed her again.

Her eyes opened—those gorgeous hazel eyes I'd seen the first night in the brothel. I knew her answer; she didn't have to speak a word.

Her eyes darted from me to the ring and I placed it on her finger. "Yes, Pat. Oh, my God. I never thought you'd propose. Not ever. I didn't even think you wanted a girlfriend. You're crazy, but I love you. Yes." She climbed in my lap and pushed me over. Our lips met and she showered me with kisses.

She stopped kissing me and grinned in such a silly way, it shocked me.

We stood up and I scooped Gabriel up. "Gabriel, do you want me to be your daddy?"

"Pat Daddy?"

I held on tight to him. One day, I would have to tell him the truth, that I'd killed his father. That his father had stolen his mom and abused her. I had the stupid thought to compare it to Luke Skywalker, who was still a good man, despite having Darth Vader as an evil father.

"Planning. I can't wait to start planning. When do you get back from your next deployment? It will take at least a year to organize. Don't worry; my dad will pay for everything."

Here we go. Of course, I knew all women wanted to plan their dream wedding. Enough of Annie's dreams had been taken away; I didn't want to burst another. But over my dead body would I let her father pay one penny.

"That's the catch. We are only going for three months this time, but I will have another mission right after that. And we have to get married before I go or you and Gabriel won't get any benefits. I want to start the adoption before I leave. I need you both taken care of and you're nothing to the military if there isn't a marriage license to back it up. The SEAL wives will welcome you, and their husbands who aren't deployed will be there if you need anything. I leave soon. I want to spend as much time with you as my wife as possible. Let's go now."

"Now. Here? Today? Without my family? They've been through enough without me and now you want to elope?"

I wanted to tell her exactly what her parents thought of her. But I'd take that secret to my grave. Maybe one day she would learn the truth—but it wouldn't be from me. No way in hell.

"Yes. Let's go to Harrah's. Now. I can't wait, Annie. I don't think you understand the SEAL community. We will have a ton of paperwork to fill out, have to get your ID card, all your benefits, and my life insurance. Get on the housing list; since I'd rather you live on base where they can keep you safe. This is the only way it will work. I can't be deployed and have you back home without a safety net. There's an eighty percent divorce rate but I won't let us be a statistic. I'll never cheat on you, you don't have to worry about that. But it won't be easy. Though, compared to what you've been through it should be a piece of cake."

"But my parents—"

I stopped her with a kiss. I didn't want to hear about her parents. I needed to protect her from them.

She paused, her lip caught in her teeth, then smiled. "Now. Let's do it."

This was the only way I could protect her. Seeing her happy face replaced the image in my head of the sad girl in the brothel and brought me peace. I rarely had peace or even desired it. My fucking bumper sticker read "Give War a Chance".

We finally made our way back down the trailhead, found my truck, and drove off toward the Douglas County Administration Building to get our wedding license. Annie called en route and we were able to get an appointment, and the chapel had an opening in an hour. Getting our license didn't take long, and we drove to a jewelry store to get wedding bands.

I picked out a small white gold one for her to match her engagement ring and she bought me a titanium band. She seemed to love her engagement ring, even though I couldn't afford to get her a huge rock. I never lived beyond my means. Annie had to be happy with life as a Navy wife. There would be no luxurious vacations and no beachfront mansions. But she'd never starve and I'd always provide for her; she knew that.

I didn't feel nervous. I was fucking sure about it. Once I made a decision, I never wavered.

The attendant signaled that we were next. The chapel overlooked the lake.

Annie pulled me aside. "Are you sure you want to do this?"

"Positive."

"I never thought I'd get married. I used to think that even if I escaped, no man would ever love me, or my son. That I'd always be Star. I'd always be seen as nothing but a whore. Then I met you and you gave me hope. Not hope that you would love me; I didn't love myself. Just hope that I would one day get my life back. Even after you saved me, I didn't think there could ever be a chance for us. You seemed so tough, so strong, and so invincible. And you're sexy. I mean, you look like an action movie star. You could get any girl, why would you want me?"

"I've always wanted you. Even though I fought it. I felt so guilty about hiring you. And I never saw you as Star. That's why the first night I asked what your real name was."

She touched my face. "See. You're the only person who I'm positive doesn't see me like that. But you constantly said over and over that you didn't want a relationship until you retired. I figured the kiss on the boat meant you were taking pity on me."

"Never, I just couldn't let—"

She silenced me with a finger on my lip. "When you told me at my house that we shouldn't see each other again, I thought that was it. You crushed me. And I was actually trying to make peace with living in a world without you in it. I focused on getting strong and healthy. Seeing you returning from deployment was bittersweet, because I didn't think you wanted to even get to know me. I don't know what switched inside your head, but you've made me the happiest woman ever. I'm so happy you chose me in the brothel. Every day in captivity I played the 'what if' game. What if I hadn't gone to Aruba? What if I hadn't been drunk that night? What if I hadn't left my room that morning? There are no more 'what ifs' in my life. I'm present. I'm here now. And if I could go back in time and choose not to get kidnapped, I wouldn't change a thing. Honestly. Because that nightmare brought me Gabriel. And to you. To think you were living in San Diego when I was in high school and we never met. We are meant to be together. Forever. I'll spend every day of the rest of my life trying to make you happy."

"I love you and promise to take care of you and Gabriel for the rest of my life." I didn't cry, but I did choke up.

The officiant came back to the center of the chapel and started the ceremony.

Annie glowed. We both held Gabriel's hands as we stood in front of the altar. We were dressed in our hiking clothes, but this was our wedding, our way. I'd give her the wedding of her dreams when I returned from deployment. But I'd pay for everything, and her parents wouldn't be invited.

"Do you, Patrick Joseph Walsh, take this woman whose hand you now hold, to be your true and wedded wife; and do you solemnly promise before God and these witnesses to love, cherish, honor and protect her, to forsake all others for her sake; to cleave unto her, and her only, with her forever until death shall part you?"

My heart pounded in my chest. "I do."

"Do you, Analía Rose Hamilton, take this man who now holds your hand, to be your true and wedded husband; and do you solemnly promise before God and these witnesses to love, cherish, honor and protect him, to forsake all others for his sake; to cleave unto him and him only, and him forever until death shall part you?"

Annie beamed. "I do."

We exchanged rings. And then I heard the words I was waiting for.

"Therefore, by the power vested in me by the laws of the state of Nevada, I pronounce you husband and wife. You may now kiss your bride."

I cupped Annie's face and kissed her. She

jumped on me and I twirled her around.

"I present to you for the first time, Mr. and Mrs. Patrick Walsh."

Annie was mine now. Gabriel was mine. I was a father. Forever. We all shared the last name of Walsh. And no one would ever hurt my wife and son again.

37. Annie

I GLANCED DOWN AT THE ring on my finger. I was a married woman now. I never thought any man would love or accept Gabriel and me. But Pat loved me; I knew he did, not just from his words, but from his actions.

We'd celebrated all day on the lake, playing in the sand on the beach. Gabriel loved Pat. And though I hadn't been able to choose Gabriel's birth father, I had just given Gabriel the best gift of all. I'd chosen him the best father for life. Pat accepted Gabriel as his own. And it made me love him even more.

Patrick began Gabriel's bedtime routine as I snuck up to the bedroom. I felt more nervous than ever. Despite my proclamations that I was healed, would I shut down during sex? Push him away, cry from pain instead of pleasure?

I drew myself a hot bath and slipped in. Strawberry scented bubbles filled the tub, and I relaxed into the suds. Tonight was a new beginning for me. I would wash my past away.

I heard the bedroom door creak open. I didn't want to wait another minute. I let out the water, exited the tub, and slathered on some lotion. A white silk camisole and matching panties beckoned me. I glanced at my body in the mirror. All the years I'd been taken, I'd hated myself. But now, I really saw myself as beautiful. I was a wife, I was a mother. I wasn't dirty, I wasn't a whore. And I couldn't wait to make love to my husband.

I exited the bathroom. Patrick sat on the edge of the bed, and he just stared at me. "God, you're perfect. I love you, Mrs. Walsh. You're all mine now."

I focused on him. His beauty, his strength. His muscles sculpted from carrying boats over his head, pushing logs on the beach. Rugged and real, he was mine. I undressed for my husband, slowly, his blue eyes following my every move.

I placed my arms around his neck, his masculine scent driving me wild. His lips traveled from my face, to my ears, to my neck. We kissed, slowly, emotionally.

I wanted him to feel how much I loved him. I tugged at his belt, and pulled off his shorts.

He stopped and reached for a condom. But condoms seemed dirty to me, reminded me of being back at the brothel. I pushed it out of his hand.

"Babe, I want to feel every inch of you inside me. Please, make love to me."

He seemed almost hesitant as I took off his boxers. I leaned in to take him into my mouth, but he pushed me away.

A look of shame crossed his face. "No." He placed his hand on the swell of my back, kissed my lips. "Come here."

I climbed on top of him, grinding my hips into his. His hands cupped my ass, steering my movements, pushing me toward pleasure.

He nuzzled his head into my chest, licking, sucking, rubbing my nipples. No more teasing. I couldn't wait any longer; I wanted to feel him inside of me.

"Now, I want you now. Please, don't make me wait any longer."

I needed him. All of him. Completely.

We were face-to-face, bodies intertwined. He slowly guided me onto him, staring into my eyes. I gasped as I felt his hard cock penetrate me. But my fear went away. There were no flashbacks. We were finally becoming one. After all the nights of longing, apart, we'd made our way back to each other. This man, my husband, loved me. He kissed my face, went slow, and let me control the motion, the need.

He kissed my nipples. Then stopped, cupped my chin and looked me in the eyes. "I love you, baby."

My confidence rose. This wasn't some cheap sexual encounter. He was now the father of my child.

He sucked on my nipples as I rode him, I couldn't get enough. Slow and shallow at first, then fast and deep. Every push and pull felt incredible. His big arms, his sexy chest, he was so goddam sexy. I was so fucking wet, there was a deep throbbing in my belly, in my soul. Faster, deeper, every thrust, every moan, brought me closer to Pat. "Pat, oh-my-God. Pat."

"Come for me, baby."

His words took me over the edge. I was almost there, but I held back, wanting to stay at this pleasure point for as long as I could. My hips bucked, I thrashed on him, rocking on his hips, little circles and twists, my core on fire.

"Pat, you're so fucking incredible. OhmyGod. Pat." I came, again and again, his body steady, waiting out my pleasure. Euphoria overtook my body, and he finally exploded inside me. Filling me with such joy. This was the most amazing high ever, even better than heroin.

"I love you, Annie. Finding you was the best thing that ever happened to me."

I collapsed onto the bed. For once, I didn't need to explain my feelings, my emotions. I cuddled up into my husband's strong embrace, and he rocked me to sleep.

38. Patrick

A FEW DAYS LATER, I woke up with her in my arms. Her head was tucked under my chin and she was curled up in front of me, leg thrown over my thighs and hair strewn across my pillow.

I wrapped an arm around her waist and pulled her closer to me. I needed the connection that only she was able to provide. The movement startled her and her eyes shot open and she gasped. When she realized it was me, her body relaxed and she gave me a sleepy smile.

"Good morning."

"Morning."

"What time is it?"

"It's early. I didn't mean to wake you."

"That's okay." She snuggled closer and kissed my jaw line. "This is nice. What do we have planned today?"

"Well, I figured we could stop by my mom's on the way back to San Diego, say hi. I haven't called her since I got back and she would probably want to know her baby boy has gotten himself married to a beautiful woman, and has a son."

She jerked backwards. "You haven't called your mom since you've been back? Patrick Walsh how could you!" She paused, then her eyes widened and she rolled out of bed. "Oh, my God, I have to get dressed."

I grabbed for her, but she pulled away and started babbling to herself as she sorted through her things. "Baby, come on. She's not going to care what you look like, I promise."

"Says you. Of course, she's going to care what I look like. I can't meet your mom for the first time looking like a mess."

She grabbed a pile of things and headed toward the bathroom, but I jumped out of bed and stopped her. "All she will see are the same things I see when I look at you. Someone who is strong, loyal, and kind. I don't want you to freak out about this. Trust me; she will think you're the best woman on Earth."

Tears filled her eyes and I crushed her to my chest. "Please, don't worry," I told her. "She's going to love you. You look beautiful in anything."

Later, we pulled up to my childhood home. It

looked the same, and even though it was a dump, it was home to me. My mom had scraped and saved all her money to buy this place so I could have a permanent home.

My mom ran out the door, her hair with a few more gray streaks than the last time I saw her. "Pat, I'm so happy you're home. Is this your new girlfriend?"

When I called to tell her I was coming by, I'd simply told her I was bringing someone special. I owed it to my mom to tell her in person. "Mom, this is Annie. Annie Walsh. And our son, Gabriel."

My mom clutched my arm. Her eyes immediately darted to Annie's left ring finger and then to her belly. "You eloped and didn't tell me? Pat, how could you?"

"Sorry, Mom. I proposed last week and we got married that day. I wanted to do it before I deployed again and we were in Nevada. We'll have a big wedding later."

My mom and I had always been close. She knew my views on marriage and that I would never ever enter into it lightly. I'd been raised to respect women. Even if I had veered off course. "I'm a grandmother?" She knelt down and hugged Gabriel. "Is there another baby on the way?"

"Jesus, Mom. No. She's not pregnant." At least I didn't think she was. We hadn't been using protection and we'd been making love every chance we could.

Annie stood by my side. Her own parents were so icy. I figured she didn't even know what to say to my mom.

"Well, come inside." My mom hugged Annie. "Welcome to the family. I always wanted a daughter and a grandson."

"It's an honor to meet you, Mrs. Walsh."

"Please, Annie, call me Tracy. Or better yet Mom, if you feel comfortable. I have to get to know the woman who tamed my son. Gabriel, do you like trains?"

We went inside and sat on the sofa. My mom found one of my old train sets and set it out for Gabriel. She had prepared all my favorites: meatloaf, mashed potatoes, zucchini boats, and chocolate chip cookies. All from scratch.

Annie went into the bathroom to freshen up, Gabriel was watching television, and my mom pulled me inside the kitchen.

"Patrick Joseph Walsh, she is the Annie Hamilton, isn't she? The girl from all the news stories who ran away from her family?"

I could never lie to my mom. "Yes. But that story was a cover up by her parents. She was kidnapped and forced into sex slavery. Gabriel is her child by the man who'd kidnapped her."

Her mouth dropped. "Are you serious? I never believed the story on the news. There'd been sightings of her, even pictures on some escort website."

My mom lived for true crime stories, people who vanished without a trace, unsolved mysteries. She probably knew more about Annie's disappearance than I did. "Pat, were you the one who saved her?"

"Yes."

I don't know how most moms would react to finding out their son had married a former prostitute, even if the girl had been kidnapped. But my mom wasn't most moms.

"I'm proud of you, son. You're a great man."

I winced. I'd left out the part that I'd hired Annie in the brothel. My mom didn't need the details. She'd be disgusted by me.

"As a woman, I'm even prouder of the fact you can love her and look beyond her past. Not many men would be able to do that and treat her with respect. And love another man's child." Her eyes looked pained. I knew she always felt guilty, that it was somehow her fault that I never had a dad. "She's lovely and so is my grandson. I love you."

"Love you too, Mom."

Annie emerged and sat down on the sofa. My mom brought out old photo albums and decided to embarrass the shit out of me.

"Here's Pat with his favorite teddy bear."

Annie loved the old pictures. I just sat back and watched her bond with my mom. If I'd taken the reward money her dad offered, I could've bought my mom a new house. I wished I could take care of her, maybe even move her down to San Diego so she could be close to Annie and Gabriel when I was gone.

"So what was Pat like as a kid?" Annie asked, with a gleam in her eye.

"Pat was very sweet and sensitive. Very attached to me. Loved trains and dogs. Always tried to protect me."

"So, pretty much exactly how he is now."

I laughed. "I'm hardly sweet."

"You are, too. And super romantic. He remembers everything I say. Then he stores it in his brain and when I'm not expecting it—bam! All my dreams come true."

My mom was eating this up. I rarely had the chance to spend quality time with her anymore, so I think getting a glimpse into my adult life was fascinating to her.

After humiliating me a bit more, Mom finally put the albums away. We put Gabriel to sleep.

"Well, Annie," Mom said, "it's been a pleasure. Please, you're welcome in my home anytime. When Pat deploys, I hope you'll come up here and visit me. I want to get to know my daughter-in-law and my grandson."

"I'd love that."

They hugged, then my mom turned to me.

"I love you, Patrick. I'm so proud of you."

"Love you, too."

Annie and I went to my childhood room and

snuggled up in bed. My Little League awards were still on the shelves, a cheesy poster of a topless Britney Spears wearing nothing but white cotton panties trimmed with pink lace hung on the wall. Exactly as I had remembered.

Annie glanced around the room. Probably wondering why my room was stuck in a time warp and hers had been turned into a museum. "I love your mom. She's so different from mine. Sweet and warm."

This was my opportunity. I had to tell her. But I couldn't. She seemed so happy, and I didn't want to ruin it.

"She's your family now. And she means it—when I'm gone, if you get lonely, fly up here. She'll take care of you and Gabriel. I need you to promise me you'll come see her."

"Of course, I will." She kissed me. We laid there a while in the dark. "Pat, I'm worried about telling my parents we eloped. You're coming with me, right?"

Damn straight. She wasn't setting foot in that house without me. And if my talk with her father went as I expected it would, I doubted she'd ever see them again. "You can count on it."

She drifted to sleep in my arms. Before I met Annie, my only goal in life was to survive and protect my fellow men. But now, my attention was split. I felt torn by my desire to protect her and loyalty to my Team. Maybe this is why I'd always felt the Navy didn't want the SEALs to have wives or families, despite what they said about the importance of a support system. Because, if I had to choose between my Team and Annie, without a doubt I'd choose her.

39. Patrick

I WOKE THE NEXT MORNING to the sound of Gabriel singing Thomas the Train songs. Annie was missing from my bed. I threw on some clothes and followed the scents of coffee and bacon into the kitchen.

After breakfast, I'd planned to show Gabriel and Annie around my town.

"Why don't you two newlyweds sneak away? I can take Gabriel to the river train. I want to bond with my grandson."

I looked at Annie. We hadn't been alone—like ever. Except that hour on the beach in Coronado.

"It's fine, Mom. We can all go to the train together." I didn't feel right leaving Gabriel alone. I trusted my mom, but he didn't know her.

Annie put her hand on my thigh. "Gabriel will be fine. Don't worry about him. Let's get out of here."

"Relax, Pat. I raised you; I can watch my own grandson. We will have fun."

"Fine, Mom. Call me if you need anything. We'll be nearby."

Annie and I said goodbye to Gabriel, and left.

I didn't have a fucking clue where to take her. "I'll show you around Sacramento."

Annie had a glint in her eye, she licked her lips. "I have a better idea. Let's go to a hotel."

Didn't have to ask me twice. "Sounds like a plan."

Blood rushed through my body, my mind went wild. Yes, Annie was my wife. And we'd made love every day since we'd been married. But I couldn't help but hold back. Gabriel was always around, and I was still paranoid about Annie having flashbacks. All my fantasies about her just didn't seem right knowing about her past. My only goal was to make her happy. So our lovemaking had been sweet, tame, loving. Incredible, emotional, intense. But I wanted to get raw, dirty, nasty. Did she?

I tossed the valet my keys. Annie wrapped her body under my arms, stroking my leg, nuzzling my neck. We walked up to the reception desk, Annie's hands all over me.

"Welcome to the Sacramento Hilton. Do you have a reservation?"

"No, we don't. Just a room for the night, please."

Annie whispered into my ear, "I want you. I can't wait for you to touch me. Fuck me."

The middle-aged clerk with mousy brown hair pulled into a tight bun raised her eyebrow at us.

Annie was giggling, kissing me. I kept my cool and handed the clerk my credit card.

I couldn't race to the room fast enough.

When we arrived on our floor, I scooped Annie in my arms. I never had a chance to carry her over the threshold. The first time we'd made love, was about me making sure she was okay, not traumatized. Now, I wanted to fulfill her fantasies.

I placed her on the bed, about to kiss her. But she had other ideas.

She pounced on me, wrapping her arms and legs around me.

Game time. I'd been dying to take control.

I shoved her against the wall, pinning her wrists above her head. She writhed in my grasp. My lips took hers, not loving kisses; we'd had enough of those. Strong, desire, lust. It wasn't sweet—it was primal, raw. Mine, she was my woman.

Before I could go further, I had to tell her something. "You have to promise to let me know if you are okay."

"Shut up, Pat, and fuck me."

Yes, ma'am. Her words went straight to my cock. Our kisses were frenzied, frantic. Her hands dropped to my belt, she pushed my jeans to the floor. I hiked up her skirt, rubbed her wet pussy through her panties.

"Pat, baby, don't stop."

I had no intention of stopping. I slid her panties off but kept her heels on. A wicked smile across her face melted me.

I knelt beneath her, dying for a taste. My mouth attacked her lips, plunging into her wet flesh. Her hips arched and she gasped. My fingers pressed up inside of her. She was so moist, so tender.

Her grip tightened on my hair, and she pulled me up.

I turned her toward the wall, one hand on her clit, rubbing her warm pussy.

I paused for a second, just to glance at her again. We needed this moment; I needed reassurance that she really wanted me like this. She squeezed my hand, and I knew she was present.

I slid my cock into her. She let out a long moan. My hands cradled her fine ass, every thrust, every push, bringing me closer to her core.

"Pat, oh my God. You're so hard, baby. Don't stop fucking me."

I fucked her deeper, faster. Every time she let out a pleasure filled sigh, it almost sent me straight to the edge. I cupped her breast with one hand and pressed her clit into my other hand.

"You feel so fucking good baby. You're so wet."

Her pussy clenched around me and released. It was so fucking hot.

She gasped, I knew she was close. She dug her nails into my thighs. "I'm going to come baby."

"Mine, Annie. You are mine. Forever. I fucking love you." I had intended to keep the love talk out of it, but I didn't care. I was so sprung on her, on my wife. The safety, the love, the comfort. Knowing that no man but me would ever touch her. That I trusted her. I knew that when I left on this deployment, she wouldn't cheat. I'd never felt that security.

I turned her to me, wanted to see her beautiful face, watch her mouth curl as she came. I threw her onto the bed, and climbed on top of her. Her hair was wild, her face was flush. A blanket of joy washed over her face.

She rocked her hips up on mine, taking me in deeper with every thrust. Licking her nipples, kissing her neck, my cock throbbed. Her pussy was so wet, so swollen, so hot.

"Fuck, Annie. Come for me, baby."

"Pat, ohmyGod. Yes."

Her pussy clenched on my cock.

"Annie!" I cradled her through her orgasm. She came again, and again. Her pussy crashed down on me and I let myself go.

It wasn't about the sex; I loved her no matter what. But I never thought we'd get here. I never thought we'd be able to have a normal sex life, that I'd always have to be careful with her. Knowing that we could fulfill all of each other's fantasies, without having her flash back, made me love her even more.

When we finally separated, my body shivered. For once, our roles reversed, she turned to comfort me. "You okay?"

I touched my wife, kissed her on the neck. "No, Annie. I don't want to leave you. I can't imagine being away from you."

"You'll never be away from me. When I was waiting for you to come back for me, I just focused on your energy. I felt your presence. We are connected. Deeply. We will never be apart."

For the first time in my life, I imagined a life outside of the Teams. Being a SEAL was the only thing I'd ever wanted to do. I thought marrying her would make it easier for me to go, knowing she was taken care of. But I had no desire to go a day without my wife and child by my side.

40. Patrick

AFTER WE LEFT MY MOM'S house, we spent a day in Marin County and then took scenic Highway 1 along the coast back to San Diego. I couldn't wait to come back from deployment and plan a real honeymoon with Annie. No Caribbean getaway, that was for sure. We talked about spending time in Carmel-by-the-Sea, Half Moon Bay, Big Sur, and Santa Barbara. With Gabriel, of course.

Annie wanted to go straight to her parents' house. I debated convincing her to wait a few days, but I'm sure she'd fight with me. That was fine. I wanted to get this over with.

I dropped Gabriel and Trigger off at Kyle's house. I didn't want Gabriel near Annie's dad, and luckily she didn't protest. Gabriel was my son now, and I would protect him. Annie called and told her parents we'd be stopping by for her to pick up the rest of her stuff.

My mind raced. I had to be smart and watch what I said. I'd given Matt my word. I was leaving in a few weeks and I wanted to make sure her father was out of her life.

Before I met Annie, I'd planned to apply to the world famous SEAL Team Six, known as DEVGRU. They were stationed in Virginia Beach and it would be great to put distance between Annie and her dad. I'd just become eligible—they required five years of stellar service in the Teams and the selection process took six to eight months. But those SEALs were the real badass SEALs, the ones who took down Bin Laden during Operation Neptune Spear. It would mean more time training, even less time with Annie. But it was a career goal of mine. I would make my decision once I came back from this next deployment, and I knew Annie would support my choice one hundred percent.

The gate opened to Annie's parents' house. Last time I came here, I was nervous. This time, I was pissed.

Let's roll.

We walked up the stairs to the front door. Before Annie could get out her key, the door opened. Her dad stood in front of us, with his nostrils flaring.

"What are you doing here, Annie? I told you not to set foot again in this house as long as you were seeing him."

What the fuck? I glared at Annie. I guess we both kept our secrets to protect each other.

"I'm not seeing him, Dad. I'm married to him. He's my husband."

Annie's mom popped around the corner; her eyes bugged out of her expressionless face. "Annie! Baby. How could you elope?"

I still couldn't figure her mother out—did she know her husband had found her "baby" and left her there to die? Of course, this was the woman who couldn't wait to redecorate Annie's room. My impression was she cared more about her image than her own daughter, but what did I know?

Annie's dad didn't even acknowledge his wife. "Mr. Walsh, I'd like a word with you."

"My pleasure." I'd like a word with him, too. I'd also like to put a bullet in his head.

The asshole took me into his office this time. I'm sure he had a gun under his mahogany desk. I wasn't worried; my weapon was concealed and accessible.

He sat in his black leather chair and poured himself a shot of whiskey from the bottle on his desk.

He bared his teeth at me. "I thought I told you to stay away from Annie. You trying to get more money out of me, boy? Name your price. Then you can tell Annie you made a mistake and get an annulment."

"I don't have a price."

"Fine, you leave me no other choice than to report you for visiting a brothel. Your career will be ruined and I'll make damn sure you're kicked out of the Teams."

I cocked my head. This guy not only left his daughter and grandson to live in hell, but wanted to ruin any chances she had of happiness. I wasn't threatened. "No, you won't. Because I'm not the only one with a secret. I know everything about exactly how hard you tried to save Annie. Do the words Neptune Group mean anything to you?"

His posture slumped and he ran his hands through his hair. "I don't know what you think you know, but you're wrong. I tried everything to save her. They couldn't find her; that's the God's honest truth."

"You can lie to me all you want, but we both know you left her there to die. Why? Because you were embarrassed about Gabriel? How can you not love him? He's your grandson. I'm not an idiot; something didn't sit right with me. We have eyes everywhere, remember that."

Eyes steady, he squeezed the whiskey glass, and his knuckles whitened until I was certain something was going to break. "How dare you, you cocky son of a bitch! Come into my house and threaten me? No one would believe you."

I laughed. "Try me."

"What do you want, Walsh?"

"Simple, and it won't cost you a penny. Stay the fuck away from my wife and son. If I hear you so much as text her, I'll come after you. I'm not sure if your wife is in on this, but if she reaches out to Annie, that's fine. I'm making this easy on you. Tell Annie you can never accept me as her husband and make her choose between you and me. She'll choose me. The only reason I'm not telling Annie the truth is to protect her, not you. It would crush her, and she's been through enough. I refuse to add to her pain. I'm deploying soon, but Annie will be safe here with my buddies. If I find out you try to hurt her or Gabriel in any way, you won't live to regret it. Understood?"

He nodded but wisely remained silent.

"Good talk." I walked out of the room. Annie's mom was talking to her about throwing a wedding reception.

"Come on, Annie. Let's go."

"Already? I haven't packed my stuff."

"I'll buy you new stuff."

Annie's dad walked out of his office. I gave him a stern look.

"He's right, Annie. Leave. We don't want to see you again. I can never accept Pat into this family. You made your choice when you married him. You're dead to us."

He must've been relieved—after all, he'd already declared her dead once before.

Annie bit her lip, but she didn't break down. It was almost as if she expected this.

"I love Pat and if you can't accept him, I don't care. I learned to live without you once, I'll do it again. Sometimes I think you both wish I never came back. I was worth more to you dead than alive. Pat's the only one who loves Gabriel and me. Don't ever contact me again."

She clutched onto me and we walked out the front door. I hoped we never had to see them again.

We got into my truck and cruised down to my place. She looked out the window the whole way. Not a single word came from her. I didn't know what to say.

Finally, I offered, "I'm sorry, Annie."

"It's not your fault. I meant what I said in there. I love you and I don't care what they think. He'll never accept you, and he always acted weird around Gabriel."

I placed my hand on her thigh. I was all she had now. I wasn't one of those men who wanted to isolate his woman from her family and friends. I wished Annie's family were decent people and I was fine if she wanted to maintain contact with Chris. But as long as I lived, no one would ever hurt Annie or Gabriel again.

41. Annie

I DIDN'T SHED A TEAR as Pat drove away from my parents' house. Why the fuck should I care what they thought about my husband? Pat was the one who rescued me. Pat was the one who treated Gabriel as his own, not some bastard child to be hidden.

Yes, Pat made a mistake by going to the brothel. He knew now hiring a hooker was wrong. He was lonely. But one truth I learned during my time as a prostitute was that all men were not bad. It wasn't always about sex. Sometimes it was just about companionship, warmth, and affection.

What would my new life look like? Everything was fine now, while he was here. But he would be gone soon. And we'd be alone. I knew I could handle it, I promised Pat I could.

I was scared. What if Pat was killed on his next

mission? I couldn't imagine losing him, losing our newfound happiness, just as we started our life together.

I finally understood all of Pat's deep concerns about marriage to a SEAL. I'd been through enough pain and anguish in my life. I had to believe, I did believe that true happiness was in store for me. That Pat would be returned to me safely, and we would have a long and happy marriage.

I'd stopped making plans for the future years ago. In the brothel, I lived in the past. Since I'd been home, I'd lived in the present. But now, I was brave enough to finally live not only in the present, but also plan for my future.

I wasn't perfect—by far. I had a long way to go still in my healing process. But having Pat's unconditional love helped me love myself.

42. Patrick

IT WAS FIVE A.M. ON deployment day. I didn't know exactly how long I'd be gone, but I knew it was at least three months. Annie and I had spent a great couple of weeks together. We were assigned wonderful housing off-base in Point Loma, near Liberty Station. It was a three-bedroom townhouse with a small yard for Trigger. We made Gabriel a great Thomas the Train room and I'd been taking him to soccer and swimming. I introduced Annie to all the SEAL wives and, of course, they loved her. They saw her just how I did, as a strong woman. The SEAL wives had promised to keep her busy while I was away. Maybe I'd been wrong about marriages in our community. Yes, most fail. But the ones that worked were because of the strongest, most loyal women. And I knew Annie was the strongest of them all.

Annie enrolled in college again. She was majoring in sociology, which sounded depressing and useless to me, but who was I to judge? I had a high school diploma and no need for a college degree. Annie also threw herself into yoga and volunteering at the animal shelter. Our love grew deeper by the day, and for the first time since I'd become a SEAL, I dreaded deploying. I hated the thought of leaving her and my son.

Kyle and Vic would be deploying with me. They were both still tragically single, which was ironic since I was the one of the three of us who'd been the most dead-set against a relationship.

Annie stood outside on our tiny balcony. The breeze blew her hair off her face. She was wearing a sundress that showed off her tan skin. She looked up to me, and her crooked smile, which I'd first noticed in the brothel, melted me.

"I'm going to miss you, Pat," she whispered, careful not to wake Gabriel.

"Me too." I kissed her slowly. I needed this kiss to take me through a long deployment.

Her arms wrapped around me. She held me tight, and nibbled my ear. I loved it when she did that. She reached out, grabbed my hand and led me to the bedroom.

I was about to undress her and make love to her for the final time before I left. But she stopped me and knelt in front of me on the bed.

She took me in her mouth, and I gasped. I hadn't let her go down on me since the night in the brothel. I still felt guilty about that day. It changed our lives forever, for the best, but I couldn't shake the guilt. I hired her. I used her.

I stopped her and made her look at me. "You don't have to do this, Annie. Ever."

"I want to, Pat. I'm going to miss you so much it will hurt. I love you. I want to please you. I'm your wife."

She wrapped her lips around me, her tongue dancing again. My mind flashed to that night in the brothel. We'd come full circle. Same girl, same amazing technique. But this time, instead of imagining that she was my faithful, loving, girlfriend who lived for pleasing me, and that being with me even for just a few months out of the year was worth enduring the loneliness when I was gone, it was real. She was real. She was mine. She respected that being a SEAL was my calling, and she didn't want to change me.

I pushed her off me. I had something to tell her.

"Annie, I love you."

She looked me straight in the eye. "I know. I love you, too."

I meant it. I loved her.

She was no longer my mission.

She was my wife.

Epilogue. Annie

GABRIEL AND I STOOD AT the dock. We'd spent all week making Pat's welcome home sign. It was decorated with trains, American flags, frogs, and seals, the kind you found at the aquarium. In big letters it read, "Welcome home Patrick. Husband, Father and Hero."

Vic's mom and his daughter also waited with us. Poor Vic still hadn't found anyone. He was such a great guy, but he was super picky. At least Kyle was in love, or so Pat said. I'd believe it when I saw it. Supposedly, he'd fallen head over heels for a NFL Cheerleader on the USO tour, one of the San Diego Wildfire Girls. Kyle, Pat and Vic had another rescue adventure—the USO convoy hit an IED and insurgents had taken the women hostage. Unlike my rescue, this one had been all over the news. I kept my eyes glued to the television, hoping to see a clip of my husband. But they'd managed to evade the media and their names and pictures were kept out of the press. Though this time, credit was given to SEAL Team Seven. Pat said it was just another day at work, completely humble and modest. He, Kyle, and Vic tried to pretend that saving people was no different than pushing papers around in an office. I had to admit, I had a twinge of jealousy knowing that my fine-ass husband had been surrounded by beautiful cheerleaders, who no doubt wanted him. Sexy girls without horrible pasts. I found myself stalking the cheerleaders' website—eyeing the brunettes, wondering if one of them had caught Pat's eye. I knew I was being paranoid and insecure, still deep down questioning that Pat could ever truly love me. But he went out of his way to assure me how much he worshipped me every chance he got. I never doubted his fidelity.

Deployment went faster than I'd expected. Pat called every chance he could, which was around every week or so. He sent me letters, gifts for Gabriel, toys for Trigger. He was so kind, thoughtful and romantic. I thanked my stars everyday that he was mine.

Gabriel was now in preschool, and I was taking college classes. Only two, because I wanted to ease back into it. The SEAL wives had been so amazing and welcoming—always ready with a casserole or last minute babysitting.

I'd pretty much cut out my old friends, except for Chris. He was still there for me and we met up weekly. He took Gabriel surfing every week. Pat swore he was okay with it, but I knew it made him jealous that another man was playing with his son.

As for my parents, I hadn't seen them. At all. My mom had called me a few times, begging me to try to work things out with my father, but I wasn't ready. Not until Patrick was back home. I needed his emotional support and to make sure they accepted him and Gabriel before I agreed to rejoin my family.

Patrick's mom had come down to visit. I loved her—she was so sweet and warm and Gabriel adored his Granny. She'd even started looking for a job down here. Pat wanted her to move so she could be around for me when he was deployed.

"Mama. It's Daddy!"

Patrick was standing at the helm of the ship, wearing his sailor uniform, complete with the bib, tie, and bellbottoms. He had at first refused to "man the rail," but I told him how Gabriel would think it was so cool and how much it would turn me on to see him from the dock. He wanted to make me happy. I knew how much he hated that uniform, but I thought he looked sexy, the way the fabric clung to his ass. My husband was fucking gorgeous.

Pat walked down the gangplank and ran to us. I was so nervous—last time we had greeted him, I didn't think he'd ever wanted to see me again. Now, we were a family.

He lifted up Gabriel, and pulled me into his strong embrace. A kiss. Long, sweet, loving. His lips, I'd missed them so. I couldn't wait until tonight to be alone with him.

"Hey babe." He placed his hand on my belly, now swollen. I was four months pregnant. "How's our little girl?"

"She's good. Excited to have her daddy home." I'd been so nervous to tell him I was pregnant. I'd found out right after he deployed. It was so soon, our marriage, now a new baby. But Pat and I did everything on fast-forward. He was so excited for our new addition, and he went out of his way to tell me over and over how he would never treat Gabriel any different than his biological child. But I never doubted that. And he'd given me the best gift of all—he delayed his plans to apply for SEAL Team Six. He'd instead accepted a three-year assignment as a BUD/S instructor, so he would be home with me, non-deployable for three whole years! He would even be around for the birth of our baby. Kyle and Vic signed up to train BUD/S with him; those men were thick as thieves.

I was about to pepper my man with a thousand questions, kiss him some more, nuzzle his chest. But Gabriel was talking his ear off about soccer.

"Annie Hamilton?"

I turned to the voice, which had called out my former name. My former life. "Can I help you?"

A lady in a fitted red suit was standing there. Clearly not a family member waiting for her loved one. "I'm a reporter for *48 Hours*. We've been trying to locate you for months."

My number was unlisted, and I hadn't even told my parents where I lived. The only one from my past life who knew how to contact me was Chris. "Well, you found me. Can't you see I'm busy? My husband just returned home from deployment."

Pat was now alerted to this stranger talking to his wife. "Who are you? What do you want?" Jesus, back not even five minutes and Pat's protective streak was already into overdrive.

"My name is Judy Miller. We've been doing an investigation on the disappearance of Nicole Race, and we have information that a sex ring had kidnapped her. Forced her to work in a brothel. In Aruba. With you, Annie. We'd like to talk to you, have you go on record. But either way, the story is about to break."

I dropped Patrick's sign and his face went white.

"Listen, lady. I don't know what the fuck you think you know, but you better get the fuck away from my wife."

The lady eyed my son. I clutched him to my side. Fuck—she knew.

I swallowed hard. "No, Pat, wait. I'm ready." I turned to the reporter. The words overpowered my lips, just like they had that night in the brothel when I'd told Pat my name. "Nicole and I were both kidnapped and sex trafficked in the Caribbean. Nicole is dead; she overdosed on heroin."

Pat's jaw dropped; the expression I'd seen on his face when he first saw Gabriel under my covers the night he'd saved me.

The reporter shook her head. "No, Annie. You're wrong. Nicole Race didn't die. She's alive. She had amnesia, was living in a small fishing village in Venezuela, no idea who she was. A United States Marine who'd been on vacation with his buddies recognized her, and rescued her. She's on her way home to the United States now. And her memory has returned."

Holy fuck! Was she serious? I'd never seen Nicole's dead body. She'd vanished in the middle of the night and Renzo had told me that she'd overdosed. Pat held me and I collapsed into his arms.

There was no going back now. It was time. Time to heal. Time to tell the world my story.

The story of my life when I hadn't been Invincible.

When I had been Invisible.

The End

Read on for an excerpt from:

Invaluable
The Trident Code: Book 2

Alana Albertson

Invaluable

Late Summer, San Diego.

The blonde Barbie doll swayed her body to the music. She was dancing on a platform, fluorescent lights highlighting her sweaty skin. Man, she was fine. Her hips swirled around and I couldn't help but imagine them swiveling on top of me. Summertime in San Diego brought out all of the honeys. Short pink skirt, tight white tank top, with a turquoise bikini top peeking through—I wouldn't be satisfied until I saw her clothes strewn all over my floor.

My wingman for the night, Vic Gonzales, was nursing his beer. He normally wasn't my first choice, but my best buddy Pat was all wrapped up in this major drama with this chick Annie who we'd saved. Poor girl had been kidnapped during spring break and forced into sex slavery. My boy Pat hired her to give him head in a brothel in Aruba, and then she told him her name. His call to action. We were motherfucking United States Navy SEALs. There was never a question—we had to save her. Now she was safe back home in San Diego, madly in love with her savior Pat, who was acting like a love struck puppy despite swearing to us that he wasn't interested in her. Don't get me wrong, I was happy for the dude, but I missed my bro.

At least Vic could dance. So that was a plus. Pat normally would just hang out at the bar all night, drinking himself into oblivion.

I took a swig of my own beer. My eyes stared intently at Barbie. Would she smile when she caught them undressing her? I wasn't a conceited prick, but I usually didn't have any problem with the ladies. At six foot five inches tall, I towered over the other men at this club. The bars in Pacific Beach, San Diego, were packed with frat boys, surfers, Marines, and sailors. But I stood out. I wasn't just your average sailor—I was a Navy SEAL and a former NFL linebacker. I'd left behind money and fame to make a difference in the world, do something I believed in. Something I'd die for.

Barbie made strong eye contact right at me. Just what I thought—she wanted me. You never knew with these white chicks, if they wanted to date a brother. Sure everyone tried to pretend we were race blind, especially since we had a black president, but as one of only a handful of African-American Navy SEALs, I was reminded every day that I stood out.

I whispered to Vic. "I'm going in. You want her friend?" Barbie's girlfriend had long, straight, dark hair touching her ass. Tall, skinny, seemed shy. Just his type.

Vic nodded. I'm straight, but I knew Vic was a good-looking man. All of the women we met dug him—tall, dark skin, fully tatted, annoying dimples. But no matter how much they wanted him, he always found a way to screw it up. He was too respectful, too sensitive. He'd end up buying a girl a drink and then spend all night showing her pictures of his daughter, Carina. He could never close the deal.

We set our beers down and headed up to the platform. No words. I started grooving behind Barbie. She shrugged her shoulders and gave me a coy smile. I was in. I wrapped my arms around her and felt her tight little ass grind up against my cock. Life was good.

Vic also started dancing with her friend, though he kept a respectful distance from her ass. Good man, that Vic.

Barbie smelled salty and sandy, like she'd just spent the day at the beach. And the way she moved made me certain that she was a dancer. I was just hoping she wasn't the type who made her living on the pole. "What's your name, sugar?"

"I'm Sara. And this is Maya."

"Nice to meet you, Sara. I'm Kyle. This is my buddy Vic. Can we buy you ladies drinks?"

Her head bobbed with the music, not committing to a yes, but she followed me off the floor. I took her hand and we found a table outside. I signaled to the cocktail waitress to take our order—she'd be over in a second. We were regulars and she knew we were huge tippers.

I glanced at Maya, who clearly wanted to be anywhere but here. She wasn't even making eye contact with Vic or me.

The waitress came over; Vic and I ordered two beers, Sara wanted a Malibu and Coke, and Maya just asked for a glass of water. Yup. Vic definitely wasn't getting any tonight.

I turned my attention to Sara. Her blonde hair was cut in one of those crisp bobs, revealing her neck. Her tits looked real, a rarity in Southern California. "What do you do?"

"I go to state, getting my teaching degree. Right now, I work in a preschool. How about you?"

Hot for teacher. Sounded good to me. "I was a linebacker for the Oakland Raiders. On a break now. Not sure what's next." *Rule #1 about being a SEAL. Never tell anyone your job. Even if it was guaranteed to get you pussy.*

"That's cool. As long as you're happy." Most girls started asking a ton of questions once you mentioned pro football, but not Sara. Maybe she didn't care about my money and actually wanted to get to know me. That would be nice for a change.

The waitress brought us our drinks. The music boomed and I could barely hear a word of what Sara was saying. Vic was talking to Maya but both of them weren't into it. I'd had enough. Time to bounce.

I brushed Sara's hair off her face. "It's too loud in here. Say what, I live down the street. You want to go back to my place?"

Her face brightened. "I'd love that."

Sara hugged her friend and whispered something in her ear. Maya squinted her face at Sara.

I signaled to Vic to help a brother out.

Vic turned to Maya, "I'll give you a ride home."

Maya gave a reluctant nod.

We said our goodbyes, and I put my arm around Sara and led her out of the bar. The neon lights of the other bars glowed in the distance as we walked toward the beach. It always boggled my mind that a girl would honestly go home with a man whom she'd just met in a club, especially knowing what had happened to Annie. But I wasn't complaining. And let's face it—Sara was safer with me than she would be with any other man. Though there was absolutely no way she knew that. She couldn't possibly be certain that I wasn't a serial killer or a rapist.

I didn't know a thing about this chick but it didn't

matter. I was only in town for the next month before I deployed again. But she didn't need the details. All she needed to know was that I thought she was the sexiest girl in the club and I planned to ravage every inch of her body tonight.

Springtime Iraq – Nine Months Later

When I was in college, spring break had always been my favorite time of the year. Winter leave always sucked because I was cramming for finals and practicing football trying to get into a bowl game, summer vacation I'd spend preparing for the upcoming season. But spring break was the one time each year that I could escape, party in the sun and hook up without a care in the world.

Not anymore. I barely could tell what time of year it was. In Iraq, the long, hot days blended together. I was now checking out terrorists instead of sexy coeds.

But today I'd get a reprieve from my fellow smelly men. Our SEAL team was the first stop on the USO tour.

Pat, Vic, and I were on our way to greet the

plane. No idea who was on the tour—usually it was a mix of NFL players, cheerleaders and some movie stars. I'd done a USO tour myself when I played ball. Hanging out with the SEALs during Christmastime was what convinced me to leave my career behind and join the Teams. My father was a retired Marine and I'd always wanted to serve my country. It was the best decision I'd ever made.

I handed Vic the big "Welcome to Kuwait" sign and the three of us walked on the runaway to welcome the USO company. Yup, I was right—a few huge guys walked down the jetway. I immediately recognized one of them, a top quarterback. I was about to shake his hand, when Pat whispered in my ear, "Hey, isn't that 'omelet girl?'"

I looked up. Fuck my life. Sara, the girl I'd met in PB that night last summer with Vic, was walking down the jetway in a skin tight sweat suit emblazoned with a flame on the back of the jacket. Pat had nicknamed her 'omelet girl' because he'd stopped by my place the morning after I'd met her and she'd cooked us omelets. She never told me she was a professional cheerleader. A fucking San Diego Wildfire Girl—part of the hottest dance team in the NFL. Then again, I'd never told her I was a Navy SEAL. I guess we were even.

"Welcome to Iraq, beautiful."

Her pale skin turned blush and I doubted it was from the hundred-degree heat. "Kyle, what are you doing here? You're on the USO tour too? You weren't on the plane—I looked you up but all I could find out was you'd quit football. Which team are you with?"

I laughed and pulled her to the side. "SEAL Team Seven sweetheart—I don't play ball anymore. You just flew thirty-six hours to entertain me. I'm ready. Come here, baby. Give me a kiss." I hugged her and kissed her cheek. Her tight little body pressed up against me.

We hadn't ended on bad terms—she'd told me that she had to go away for a family vacation and by the time she'd returned, I'd been long gone.

An older lady with bleached blonde hair nudged Sara. Probably the chaperone. These cheerleaders usually traveled with their directors, like a modern day chastity belt. Fuck that, to get some alone time with her I'd throw a flash bang grenade if I had to. Despite her all-American good girl cheerleader image, Sara was a freak—our night together was one for the books. And I needed a repeat performance.

Her body flinched at the sound of a mortar going off in the distance. The pink sky hung above us, thick with smoke. "I can't believe you're here. I couldn't figure out why you'd vanished. I thought we'd connected." She paused and her eyes focused on my gun. "A Navy SEAL? You gave up the NFL?"

"Absolutely. I love football, but now my life has meaning. Out here, football is important to the men and women who serve. That's how we tell time. Each game means the passing of another week. Another week closer to going home." Vic and Pat stepped over to me. "You remember Vic and Pat, don't you?"

Her girlfriends now gathered to her side. There were seven other cheerleaders: a redhead, two brunettes, another blonde, a Latina girl, an Asian girl and a sister. It was like an ice-cream shop of hot women—one flavor for any taste.

"Yeah, Pat was your trainer, right?"

Pat smirked and gave her a hug. His eyes made a respectful dance around her friends, but he kept his distance. Ever since he'd married Annie, Pat kept himself in check. He didn't want any temptation. All he cared about these days was getting home to her and their son in one piece, especially now that she was pregnant.

The rest of the plane had embarked now. I grabbed Sara's luggage and escorted her and her fellow cheerleaders to the barracks. They were to stay in the Distinguished Visitor quarters—small, single rooms each with their own bed and dresser. Much better than the shithole barracks that I bunked in. With any luck, I'd be crashing with her tonight.

I placed her suitcase in the room, dust flying everywhere. "So you're a cheerleader? Girl, I knew you were a dancer."

She sat on the edge of the bed. The chin length

bob she'd rocked in that nightclub had magically grown into waist length curls. My mom was a hairdresser; I knew a weave when I saw one. "I'm still a preschool teacher. Why didn't you tell me you were a SEAL? That's awesome."

Her legs were crossed and I could see the outline of her panties through her sweats. I loved my job but I missed being around women. Their voices, their hair, their soft bodies were intoxicating.

"Don't take it personally. I don't tell anyone what I do. It's safer that way. If a guy goes around boasting he's a SEAL, he's a liar."

She was fighting a yawn but it overtook her. I knew she must've been tired, after her long travel day. I had a week to be around her, take care of her every need, and maybe she'd take care of mine. Plus I couldn't wait to see her dance in those tight white boy shorts her cheer team wore.

"I'm going to let you get some rest, but I'll be back later. I'm sorry I didn't tell you I was deploying. I figured if it were meant to be, I'd see you again. You're like an angel sent to me now. I'll take care of you while you're here and make sure you're safe." I leaned into her and gave her a kiss. Her soft lips scraped against my beard and it took every bit of control I had to pull away from her.

"I'm glad you're here, Kyle. But, just so you know, I'm seeing someone."

Of course she was. "Is he a SEAL?" I'd never sleep with another Team guy's woman, under any circumstances. Even if I didn't know him.

"No. He plays Lacrosse at state."

I winked at her. "Then he's not my problem now, is he? What happens in Iraq, stays in Iraq."

She winced. "No, Kyle. It's great to see you again, but I'm taken." The sweat from the heat made beads on her forehead. Her plump pink lips parted, begging me to kiss them.

"We'll see about that, Sara. Anyway, get a good night's rest. I'm your personal security guard for the week. I'll see you tomorrow." I walked out of the room and went back to our barracks. I didn't believe in fate—Pat and Annie were always talking about how they were destined to meet and be together. Could that be true? What were the chances of Sara and me meeting in San Diego, both omitting parts of our lives, and reuniting across the world? The cheerleader and the ex-football player—had a nice ring to it.

I woke the next day at zero six hundred and for a second I thought that seeing Sara had been a dream. Once I came to, I hurriedly got dressed. Pat and Vic were already waiting for me.

Pat slapped me on the back. "So you want me to distract, maybe kick up a sand storm so you can get some alone time together?"

"Sounds like a plan. How's Annie?"

"Good. No longer having morning sickness. Just got off Skype. We find out the baby's sex on Friday.

But I'm sure it's a boy."

Vic cackled. "In your dreams, Walsh. It's a girl and you know it."

Had to hand it to Vic—he was right. Pat had a son, but his biological father had been the man who kidnapped Annie. All Team guys ended up with girls. Something about our balls being frozen in the cold water made our sperm only shoot out Xs. One of our buddies had six daughters, six! But I'd show these fools how it was done. When I decided to have children, I'd take a month leave and head to Hawaii. Warm that shit up.

I glanced at the schedule: transfer to next base, meet and greet with NFL players, show from cheerleaders, autographs. They'd come back here after lunch and then repeat the activities here.

I ditched Pat and Vic and went to Sara's room. I needed to see her before she left on the convoy. With any luck, she'd still be asleep.

I knocked on the door, careful to keep my rap silent and not wake her fellow cheerleaders or the virgin patrol.

She opened the door, her hair wild, her eyes sleepy. She was wearing a tank top with no bra and white panties. Her nipples were erect and I wanted to suck them until she screamed my name.

"Kyle, what are you doing here? Is everything okay?" she whispered.

I shut the steel door. "Sure, babe. I just wanted to see you, alone." The walls were barren, white, thin.

She sat on her bed. "What's up? I told you I was seeing someone—"

"I know. Don't worry. I get that. I just wanted to tell you I'm sorry I didn't tell you I'm a SEAL and that I'd be gone when you came back from your vacation. I thought we had something, for real, but since I was leaving I didn't see the point."

She nodded. "It's cool. I get it. I do. I figured you'd thought I was a slut for going home with you the night we met. I don't normally do that, I swear."

All girls want you to believe you are the only man they'd hop into bed with. I didn't doubt her, but I wasn't one of those men who actually cared if she was easy since I was a player. "I believe you. But you're here now." I touched her shoulder, and watched her body shiver. I wasn't going to push myself on her, she had a boyfriend and if she weren't into me, I'd back off. But I hadn't gotten laid since we left for this deployment, and I was damned if I wasn't going to try.

Her body responded to me, her chest heaved, her mouth moistened. My hands cupped her face and I kissed her, my beard scratching her soft skin. If I was going to take this any further, I had to get her out of this room, away from this creaky bed, and the adjacent ears of her chaperone. She had a week here, so I could take my time.

"Kyle, I've thought about our night so many

times. I stalked you on Facebook and wiki. But I can't. I don't want to get kicked off the team. And my boyfriend—"

I placed my finger over her lips. "It's okay, baby. If you want to spend some time alone with me while you're here, I can arrange that. I just need you to be sure. I want you. But the ball's in your court."

She didn't hesitate. "I'm game." So much for her deep commitment to her boyfriend. She rubbed her fingers over my chest and traced down to my cock. My length grew inside my cammies and I wanted to take her then and there, but I needed to wait.

"You've got a big day. I'll work something out for later tonight. I'm going to sneak out." I kissed her and cupped her ass in my hand. I walked back to my barracks. I'd plan a date with her later. Shit, Pat owed me one. He'd find a way to hook a brother up.

Two hours later, Pat, Vic, and I helped the entire tour leave to go to the next base. There were three seven-ton vehicles in the convoy to transport the USO performers.

The girls were lined up two by two like they were going on an ark with the chaperone in back. Sara pushed to the front of the line and gave me a playful look. I hadn't been imagining it—we had a spark.

Vic loaded the girls into the body of a vehicle where a Marine would sit with them and another Marine would take position as the gunner on the top.

Everyone safely inside, a third Marine turned on the ignition and the vehicle rambled around the dirt roads. Sand flew through the sky, sprinkling on the window and we waved them goodbye.

Pat, Vic, and I headed back to our barracks. We hit the gym, and later checked in with our command.

An hour later, a Marine wire dog ran into our barracks.

"What can I do for you, devil dawg?" I asked.

"It's the convoy for the USO. There was a roadside bomb and it's been hit! Not sure if there are any casualties but we think some of the girls may have been taken hostage."

What the fuck? Pat, Vic, and I exchanged looks. No words, we loaded our weapons and headed back to our command.

I promised Sara I would keep her safe. Whoever took her, took the wrong girl. Because I would tear this country apart to find her. This is exactly why I left the NFL. *I'd never win MVP, never win the Super Bowl, but some heroes don't play games.*

AUTHOR'S NOTE

Thank you for reading my book.
If you liked it, would you please consider leaving a review on Amazon?

This second version of *Invincible* was revised and rewritten after reading all the amazing readers' and bloggers' reviews. I took in consideration every reviewers' comments and constructive criticism. Thank you from the bottom of my heart for giving me feedback so I could make *Invincible* the book the blurb deserved.

Also available by author:
Love Waltzes In
Waltz on the Wild Side
Snow Queen
Coming Soon:
The Picture of Dulce Garcia
Invaluable
Infallible
Unforgettable
If you would like to keep up on my latest news—please sign up for my newsletter on www.alanaalbertson.com

ABOUT THE AUTHOR

Alana Albertson is the former President of RWA's Chick Lit and Young Adult chapters. She holds a Masters of Education from Harvard and a Bachelor of Arts in English from Stanford. A recovering professional ballroom dancer, Alana writes contemporary romance, romantic suspense, and young adult fiction. She lives in San Diego, California, with her husband, two sons, and four dogs. When she's not spending her time needlepointing, dancing, or saving dogs from high kill shelters through Pugs N Roses, the rescue she founded, she can be found watching episodes of Homeland, or Dallas Cowboys Cheerleaders: Making the Team.
Please visit her website at www.alanaalbertson.com.

Made in the USA
Charleston, SC
19 August 2014